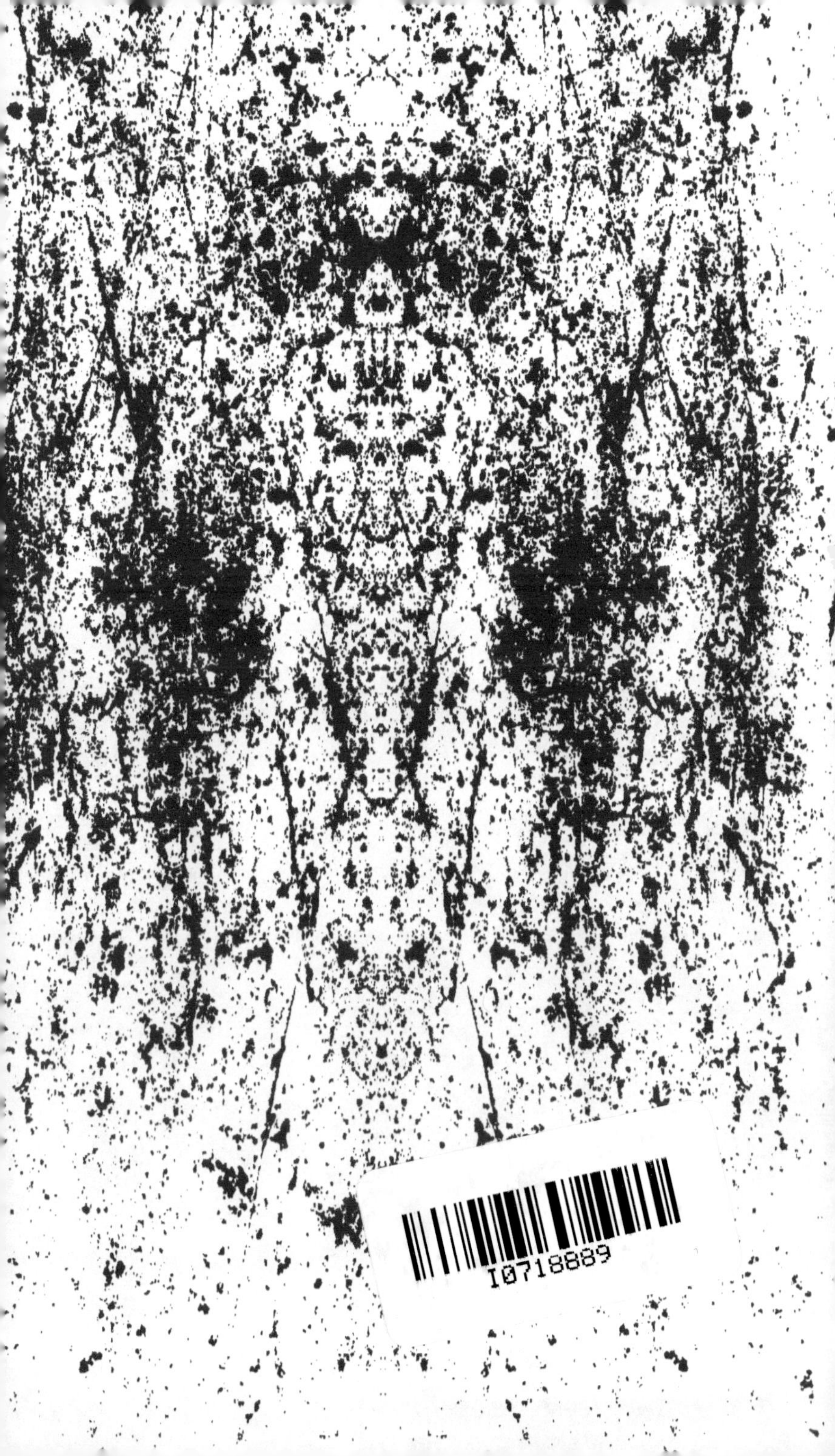
I0718889

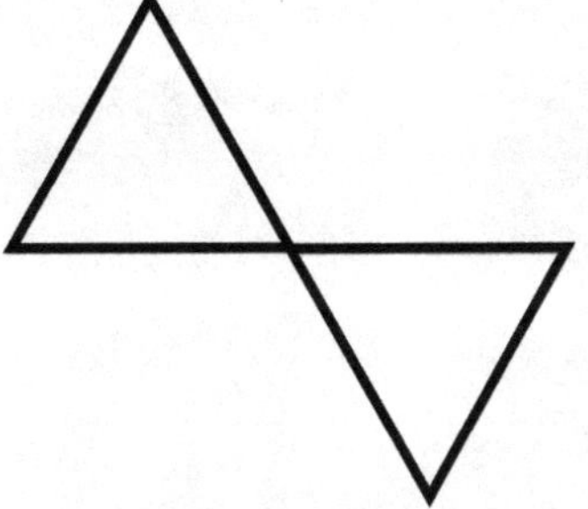

In The Vast and Boundless Deep
Kenny Mooney

__FLAT__FIELD__PRESS__

For Francesca

THE MAN OF THE TOWER

This Tower in black, this throat, this great chimney. Thrusting into sky. Punching through clouds. An arm stretching from the earth to Heaven. What light now is there in this place? Nothing is real here but what you touch. Nothing exists but what you feel. I have struggled through these dark years. Reached down my throat, into my lungs and wrenched the breath from my body, to know if it is real. To know that I do in fact lie here now, amongst these damp and destroyed plaster walls. The ruin and waste of a life's past. I suck in the dust and rank odour of this place. The churning smog that rises. This place is collapse. This place is decay. These piles of apartments heaped now like bodies into the sky. All these floors of homes, a once throbbing city in black stone. They fall. They disintegrate. And what of those who once filled this Tower? What of their movements and sounds? I wonder long about their faces. There is nothing here but their absence. Nothing but the holes they left and the stench of failure. My failure. My cold cowardice. Yes. I wake in the dark and that smell makes me sick. And sometimes I am kept warm by my anger. The few things I have left. But this servant of God does not leave his post. I have stood by the windows of these apartments, on many floors, looking out over the world, scanning for signs. And that question, should I search for them? No. What would there be to find anyway? So here I am alone, within this Tower of dark and plaster and stone. I keep the fire burning. I do my work for my God, hoping, needing, longing. His fire is fed with the books they wrote, the music they made, the films they shot, the words and ideas they dared to speak. The blasphemy of a godless age. Of science and psychology. Yes. Those lies. I can see them move their mouths and their slow smiles twist. I smell the burning of television screens, the roar of radio static. My God's voice shudders the walls of his chimney, pushes air from my lungs. They used to say that his booming was destroying our home. The cracks that we saw splitting our walls, were caused by his mighty voice. Their fear was in the darkness of their eyes, in the way they huddled in their apartments. It is their shame that blackens this place now, their betrayal that dampens the fire. A fire that is fading daily, low as I am on the fuel to feed it. I have burned and consumed so much of this place. I have given to those flames the lives of those who left, and now there is no more. The heat dissipates. I shiver in the darkness. Receding now is the loving orange embrace of his holy flame. And so I wake on this dark morning. With the cold. The dying warmth. A flicker of amber in the rooms of my home. These are days full of fading. For so many of these long years I have tended to the fire. I have burned all but my very body. Stripped this Tower clean. All for his grace. Yet here I am. A pathetic remnant, wasted and naked, lying in the rags of my bed. Amongst the filth of my useless body. I have lain here like this in the dark for so long. Feeling the fire fade, knowing there was nothing left for me to burn. Knowing soon it would be reduced to cinder and ash, and then I would truly be alone. I have lain here like this in the dark and pondered their faces. Those who chose to leave. Those who had no choice. I have questioned their motives. Shouted wordlessly into the dark. Tried to recall the shapes of their names with my mouth, so I might call them out. I have begged, arms outstretched, to their ghosts. Among their number were people I knew, cared for. Loved. Where now do those ghosts wander? Do they haunt this place? Shades drifting through the Tower, watching my movements. Plotting against me. Those blasphemers. Sinners. My rage, my abandonment. How they left me to carry on this duty alone. Here I rise from my bed and leave these rooms, out to the wrecked walkway overlooking the great throat of the Tower. Down below, what is left of the fire burns. A sea of glowing orange embers, flames rising and bursting across what was once the gardens at the centre of the Tower. I can still feel the heat, yet I know it is dying. I recall the times when those flames roared, great columns of searing orange and yellow and red. The intensity of the heat drove me to the higher floors where I scoured for fuel, throwing it over the balconies down into the pit. Now I make my home on the sixth. At one time it was the twenty-first. Gradually, as the fires have dimmed, I have moved lower and lower. To be close to his heat. For in the crackling, the hissing, lives the voice of God. Humming within the body of that fiery sound, the white noise of a carrier wave. And when you hear that sublime song all else falls away and you stand exposed before his power. And these nights as I lie in bed. As I paint the walls with scenes of sinners, their faces turned away. As I try to recall them. Their names. The voice of God comes to me in waves. Moves through me. I crouch in corners and quake in his presence. Sweat oozes down my back, thick as oil, the filth of my sin. There was a time when I tried to write down what He told me. To translate it. To understand it. But my hand became paralysed. Then my arm. My finger dripped red, my own body's ink, refusing to make the shapes I heard. But that was before I understood the nature of God. Before I understood sin. It was not always this way. Once this Tower moved only to the sound of the people who lived here. Their voices, shouts, cries, laughter flooded this place. So many floors. So much humanity, climbing. Those days we led Godless lives in the artificial light. Sinful, neon, and electric. We were selfish and deluded, interested only in flesh. Long shadows cast. We built this Tower. We mined the rock. We dug into the earth for minerals and valuables, decorating our homes with the shining, the glistening, the gleaming. As eyes those sparkles kept watch over us, a thousand million glinting points in the darkness. Our blindness. There was community. Family. A common goal we all worked towards.

The Tower. But it was purposeless. Without the guidance of God, our goal to build the Tower up was onanistic. It was sin. And yet we worked. Moved to the rhythms of an unknown system. The stone we mined was deep black and brought a chill to our hands. Those skilled in the arts favoured it for sculpture. It was a fine material to build in, and the Tower fed on this. Out of the mines, growing higher than everything else, dwarfing all of God's work. Defiance. Blasphemy. The liars' lights blinked. Pulsed. Throbbed. Strobing through the darkness. And below the Tower, the City. The vast sprawl of light and noise. Some of us came from there to the Tower, seeking refuge, an escape. Some of us left the Tower for there, tempted by stories we had heard. Of limitless pleasures. Of decadence and transformation. Stories of so many words in so many tongues. Those of us who had been born and raised within these walls, who felt the black rock within our hearts, viewed these newcomers with suspicion, and spat on those who left. We who are pure. We who feel the black rock in our bones and blood. Who sweat the dirt of the mines. None remain. None but I. And my bitterness still hisses through my teeth when I think of those. Traitors. Cool night air drifts in through a smashed window. The floor a mess of broken glass. Another shattered apartment. Empty. This is the only future I can see now for me, for the Tower. Cold and lifeless. The Tower will hang over the City, a black shard, its presence felt only by its absence. And me hanging within. Wandering forever through these tunnels, like a blind man. If only there were a way to return life to the fire. Would the people return? Would they see the light and know He is here and beg for forgiveness? And he will show them mercy. Show me mercy. I cough and spit. Taste blood. I think about that word. Mercy. Looking out into the darkness. Looking down into the City. To the burned waste that surrounds the Tower. I turn away. Return to the room. There are some scraps here and there. Some old books. Some garbage. It all goes in my sack. I sit on the debris-strewn floor—I think this was a child's room, and flip through the pages of an old worn book. The edges are blackened and scorched. At one time the heat singed everything here. I forgot how to read some years ago. Or maybe I never really knew how. Maybe I just pretended, and made up all those stories I thought I had read. Or maybe God burned those words from my mind. This book has pictures, hand drawn images of small children and animals playing. I think I had a book like this as a child. My mother— I wipe a hand across my face. Bloody smears now. And my fingers. My hands. Shaking. Nails black and broken. Blessed. Bathed in fire, I am a hymn to the power of God. All the work I do in his name. All the scars and burns and bruises, symbols of my dedication. Yes. I am an instrument of God. I move through these hallways. I gather for his good grace, to fuel the holy fires. Yes. Take a breath. Yes. Move beyond these walls. Move above these floors. Higher. Higher still, into the gaze of his love. How I long to feel the comforting warmth of his great arms. Embracing. So I gather and search. As long as possible. For his eyes watch me constantly. And I must not scrimp. I must not fall into sin. I would be banished from this place. Like the others. All the contents of my sack, emptied now over the railings, down into the pit. The fire, the hiss. Still heat I feel upon my face. Still the burning and the smell. Holding now in my hand the children's book. Of stories and pictures. Hesitation. The smell of burning plastic. Returning now to my own space. To gather myself amongst the things I have kept. That I have allowed.

My blankets and bedding. The small trinkets. The light cast by a cluster of candles. A dull yellow that softens the edges of the stone. The drawings upon the walls. Many faces around me. No photographs. No pictures. Coiled in my bedding, the book in my hands. Dirty black fingers trace over the words, seek out their shape in my mouth. I have not uttered a coherent word in years. Not since— My voice is cracked and lost, not like the voice of God. A great oceanic swell of sound. Myriad exploding stars. Like those books of science, destroyed in the beginning. The first cast into the fire. Their hollow sin. Stories of planets and galaxies and stars, claims of being higher than Heaven itself. Higher than God. No man can understand, can perceive the nature of him. Their arrogance. Those texts are what led the people of this Tower to empty lives. And how they paid. Thinking now that there is no wrong in keeping this book. There is an innocence here. The images bring a thin smile. Remind me of— And yet the raging, the roar of fire rises. I crawl to my knees, huddled to the deluge of orange flooding through my doorway. Face against the black stone floor. Black stone hewn by the hands of many hundreds, thousands. By me. Cold against my face. Yet the heat. The wrath of my God. Hands clenched, fingers intertwined, a pleading. The words try to form in my mouth, those apologies I know so well, but fail to take shape. All words lost. And the tears I have shed, coursing through the soot upon my face. Such overpowering noise. Such overwhelming sound. The urgency of his demands make my muscles twitch, and I feel my body shaking. Nodding. Yes. Now I understand. Yes. All words. All are sin. There are no exceptions. The book arcs through the air and falls, down into the flaming embrace. And I see the face of my mother. And I hear her soft words in my ears as she reads to me. Her hand upon my brow, soothing the fever. And those I have lost. The family I no longer have. That I abandoned. For my duty. A calling they did not understand. They did not accept. How could they not see, not feel, the terrible pain inside my soul, as they turned away from me, as they rejected not only my love, but the love of God? I carry their faces with me forever. I carry them in my heart, despite the great space He takes. I must pay penance for my transgression. Punishment for angering God is severe. To be out of his light. Out of his gaze. Isolated and alone. It is the thing I fear most. And there is only one place where the absence of his light is most complete. I must descend into the mine and meditate on my sins. I must crawl into the darkness. Lie there and wait. For purification within those halls. That labyrinth below. And outside. Beyond the Tower and into the hills. Down and into the ground. Away from the light of God. Away from the light of the day. The City. The sound of the Tower. Its hum. My heart thunders as I think of not feeling that thrum through my body. No heat. No fire. Just the blackness. The void. The nothing. And only my own voice, that pathetic wordless mewling. Only my own memories in the pitch. To be alone is to be truly haunted. The descent of the Tower, through the carcass of what once was, picked clean by my hunting. So many empty hallways and corridors, so many stairwells leading only to more darkness and silence. Only the sound of my own laboured breathing. Only the soft padding of my feet across the stone floors. I check apartments as I pass. Always seeking. A door gives to my gentle pressure, its surface ravaged by heat, the colour of the paint barely recognisable. I stand in the doorway. The disappointment that rises in me never fails to emerge when no voices greet me. When no laughter. I do not know why I expect it. Why I fool myself with such hopes. For a few minutes I remain. To recall who lived here. To hear their words. But they are lost. Bitter tears now. So I turn and continue down the Tower. There is enough soundless darkness waiting for me below ground, I need not dwell on how much of it makes up my life. My home. And as the flames of his fire draw closer, my body sweats, pushing out the dirt and the filth of my sin in caustic rivulets that singe the very skin on my back. I have not seen the fire this close in many years now. Not felt its touch. So perfect. The yellow and orange and red flashes like so many demonic creatures, and I gasp. I cough. Now I spit and it is black and thick. For these long moments, standing in the awesome presence of something so powerful, so alive. This is the thing I have fed, kept living. I have nurtured this as a parent tends to a child. I have raised it up to the level of my God. I have built this in his honour. For such glory. And such incredible energy. Tightening my skin. Pushing into me, moving through me. I feel that heat deep down in my lungs. A hand to my face, shielding my eyes, looking across the field of fire. All the gardens gone. All the parks and exercise fields. All the trees and bushes and plants, the many colours of flowers. All eradicated by the flame. I drop to my knees and force myself to vomit. Filthy fingers itch. In the presence of this flame, I empty myself of the dirt of the Tower. Yet I must turn away. Begin my descent. For to descend is to become pure again. In darkness there is sin, hidden, unseen. Without form. I must face and challenge my fears. In that netherworld where things both exist and do not. Where I will cease. I am a sudden curve of shadows. And outside a scene of waste. Outside is corruption and decay and rot. Moving quickly over the blackened and scorched earth, through the lines of destroyed metal hulks, their shattered windows and melted rubber, all rust and peeling paint. And the stench. Choking back the clot that rises in me, pushing against my chest and forcing the air from my lungs. This lumbering gait. A ragged breath in the darkness. The path to the mine is committed to memory. Fixed. From the years walking that same route, back and forth, dirty and black, filth ingrained in my eyes and nose. Even in this night, I would know my way. Amongst this ruin. No fear will plague me if my God is with me, in my heart. But here I am beyond his reach. And so constantly on the edge of panic. And as I get further away, I feel his presence grow weaker. And when I descend into the mine, I will be completely without him. This I know. And this is God's work, his purpose. To be excluded and removed from his sight. To be cast out into the wilderness. And tempted, yes. I must prove myself worthy of being welcomed back into his loving embrace. The Tower. Its stone. His hymn. And my fading, dying light of a home. So a need for this pestilent ground. A torture path. This way I must go. Must walk, not run. Be courageous. Be noble. And so my breathing deep. My pace even. The sun will begin its ascent into the sky before the mine shows in the hillside. And I will hold myself to a walk. Fists clenched firmly at my sides. Soon all the rot will be behind me, and before me will be clear. A calmness. Now as the first amber of dawn begins to slowly arc across the horizon, the great opening of the mine on the side of the hill behind the Tower. Hewn of the same black rock as the mighty pylon of God, but older. Ancient. Some say impossible. Always my hands on the surface. Always the caress, the touching of these symbols and shapes carved into the stonework. These cold, seamless stones. And the power contained within. The energy that flows even now. So many years. To bless myself before them. To kneel and beseech their builders, for they surely are the ones who went before me. Who uttered the name of God and called him father. To descend within these halls is as holy as rising into the heights of the Tower. Into the darkness and the enveloping silence. To feel the breath in your body frozen. To feel the sound of your voice flatten and vanish into an abyss you can barely fathom. And down into it I must journey. For how long I do not know. As long and as deep as it takes. Never have I seen the extent of these caverns. Never known their reach. Yet in them I toiled for all the years of my life. Before. And now. Returning as a new man. Enlightened. Made whole by the grace of God. They have been empty now for all the time since. All the After. Nothing stirs here. I have served penance down in these depths many times over the years. And yet it never seems to be enough for him. His voice is searing disappointment in me, the voice of my own father, his slurring, his mocking laughter. God does not mock me, of course. Yet when I sense his shame in me, I remember those eyes— But this is also a kindness. For God knows that within these tunnels, I will rediscover what brought me to his light. And yet a hesitation as the sunlight gives way to dark. A fear that this may be my last journey into the caverns. That this time a collapse may take me. Trap me. This time I may fall into one of the many shafts, their extent unknown. And fall forever. Such dreams of falling. Never ending. A scream caught in my throat. And when I wake, to sweat and piss, coughing in my entangled bedding, it takes long moments before I realise that sound is me. As familiar as I am with these tunnels, I am not so surefooted. It is as though these halls and galleries reshape themselves, shift and move. Sometimes it is as though there are new passages and rooms, spaces that did not exist before. And in this blackness my feet fail to find proper pathing, and trips come, catching me off balance. Into the dark. Out of sight of the world above. Once I would have allowed myself a lamp, to cut through the fog of black and reveal what was hidden. But God demands more conviction, and I am compelled to make my proof. And light renders all it touches real. It allows that which lives in the shadow to take shape. I must not let the sin of this place take on form. If it does, then it would escape, and all the world would fall to darkness. These rock walls run with cold. Wet hands go to my face, and I can taste the bitterness of the stone. And through the dark these walls guide, through long passages, and down, deeper into the earth. Into the rock. And as I descend, it is not only through the ground, it is through the years. Far into the past now. The many voices of those who worked the rock. The hammering and drilling. The blasting. The opening of caverns, voids in the earth, hidden until the moment dynamite shook the walls to dust. The wonders uncovered in brilliant fluorescent lighting, flickering through the mine.

And yet the search for rock, black rock. More valuable than any precious stones or gold or silver, more useful than any metal or ores. Strong enough for construction. Delicate enough for carving, and sculpture. A brilliant, shining black, almost glowing. These halls rumbled to the sound of carts, the boots of men, their shouts and laughter. Names all forgotten. All gone. Voices lost, stolen by the depths. Complete darkness now. Beyond the entrance arch, a series of passages down, through chambers and great galleries, where the space is felt in the huge expanses of air, intense cold. This is the silent place where penance can be paid. When cast in light these incredible halls are like pictures of cathedrals I have seen, drawings and etchings in the books we had before. All ash now. Standing within the heart of this place, the ceiling so high above, unseen, like the face of God, and as unreachable. These things we took for granted. We didn't understand their significance, or the gifts within. Not until it was too late. For them. I have stood in these subterranean churches and called the name of God into the dark, a wordless sound of a name—a name that no mortal can understand. I have stood here and raged for days. And the isolation. The embracing silence. It was the answer that filled my soul, pushed out the fear and the rot, which over time does gather in a man's heart. It settles there like a fine dust, sticking to the insides. My days and nights spent wandering the Tower, those years of breathing in that atmosphere. All that canker fills me. And so it is inevitable that the time comes when I stray from the path, and I find myself below ground, to flush that sickness out. And so here I push deeper into the underground night to find some salvation. Again. To find that which man has turned from and ignored. And I feel the heat of my breath around me, billowing out into these cold chambers. If I could see, it would be tumbling to the ground like ash. My volcanic mouth. So I lie here, with the hard stone against my back, prostrate and staring. Black as tar. The many tasks required of me in the Tower, duties performed in his name. When I find myself here, their sudden absence jars. The space to wonder and reflect. Back in my rooms, those moments are few and far between. No time. Must not think or dwell on— These periods down within the ancient mine, there is nothing but reflection. Within the void of dark the world gets smaller. Concentrated. There is me at the centre of a universe of dark matter and black flame. A coiling of ash encircling me. There is me reaching for something beyond reach, within the embers of orbiting debris. But it always moves beyond me. Always achingly close, never to be grasped. And so my body curls, and I hold myself close. Only within my own embrace. For hours and hours, just the sound of me. My own breathing, like some kind of creature. How long has it been since I have listened to the noise of my own body? And moving further into the mine. Further into the chill and the stone earth. Over the metal of tracks, the overturned carts left where they fell, their contents spilled out into the chambers, lumps of hard, angular rock. Bruising. Grazing. I fumble and trip as I go. And moving blindly through. Feeling of empty space before me. And a rising breath on my face. A shaft just in front of me, so deep and black. So unseen. And I pause and rest there by the edge. I listen to the breathing of the mine. These shafts were once for metal cages full of men, descending and ascending the hive. Scattered throughout, now they are still, like the airways of some huge stone creature. Throats opening down into lungs. Drawing the air down. Expelling it on the far side of the hill. There was always that stomach lurch when the lift would begin moving. The men would laugh. I would laugh. We were all afraid, but we dared not show it. To be consumed by this underground was an end unlike any other. To never be returned to the surface. To never have the light on your body. A burial so final. And there were many who went wandering in these halls, who went wandering and never returned. Forever lost. So my worry now, by the side of the open mouth into the depths. How close I had come this time. And my breath slows. I hold it for a moment. Reach out. An arm's length to the fall. Fingers delicate on the lip of the wide, yawning chasm, an edge worn so smooth it is more like flesh than stone. Against my palm as my hand slides down the inside wall. My forearm gentle over that curve. The breath that moves up from below through this shaft, I ponder its origin. From far, far below me, where many other tunnels connect. Some will open to the outside, yelling soundlessly out at the world. But the thought, a persistent image, of a great beast lurking in the far below, in the deep of this place, in slumber. I see that monster always. In waking visions during the unending night, it crawls up through the maze of tunnels and shafts. A heavy breath of poisonous gas. Huge talons claw and scrape at the walls, pulling the enormous body up. And when it reaches the massive cathedrals, it opens a pair of wings, letting out a deafening roar that rumbles through the rock, rising to the surface of the earth, cracking open the sky in arcs of red lightning. These images leave me reeling across the floors. Crashing against walls in horror moments of choked screams. Fingers scratch. Claustrophobia seizes me. Those long fits drag out, lasting hours as I scramble in the dark, desperate for an escape, an exit. But leaving the mine is not so easy. An opening presents itself when my penance is spent. Only then will I find an archway to the sky. So here now, by the open maw into the depths of this place, might the beast snatch my dangling hand and arm? On its journey up, out of the abyss, opening its terrible jaws and consuming me whole so I might dwell forever in its belly. And there—a sound now. For a moment an image of those white eyes and those claws flashes before me and I am a recoiling curl of limbs. Yet the sound is distant. So far below me. A dragging, a scraping. It starts. Stops. Carried up from below on the deep breath of the mine. And I am frozen in place. Listening and waiting. For long moments I am thundering heart and blood. Rasping breath. Dry lips and my mouth moves, opening to make some sound. Then a pause. Breathing deep, I call out into the dark of the pit. Wordless, senseless barks into that forever void. The hollow reverberation of my own broken voice, cascading around the chamber, down through the shaft below, and up above where it continues to rise. My back to the floor as that disembodied sound echoes into nothing, gradually fading. For a reply, I wait. And hope. And yet. What if I am being tested?

Tempted? I have always seen these tunnels as being out of God's sight. Beyond his reach. This is not his world. This is the lair of dark and of that coiling creature that churns so far below. The thing that causes the world to shudder. The Tower to shake. But what if He can extend himself here? Could He be testing my resolve? My commitment to him? By tempting me with another, a companion who could share my burden, one I swore to shoulder alone? And yet, never have I been tested in this manner. Not in this place. So only lies now. Only the filthy mocking of the dark. A rush of anger. Of raging. Desire to show my mettle. A blind scurry for the overturned mine cart, pushing it over the stone floor. Such a heaving, such pressure building. Feet digging for purchase. And now movement forward, and a cry that erupts to the high ceiling and comes back to me in twisted forms, demonic laughing. The cart screeching metal over rock, resisting, but my anger driving it to move. And pushing, pushing. Such snarling until. In free fall. The cart vanishes from my grasp, and I fall back to the floor, exhausted. The cart slams and crashes as it drops down the shaft, broken metal spinning and shattering. My mouth moving in shapes of laughter, the sound lost in the cacophony of falling debris. The thundering of my anger in descent. As crashing and falling begins fading into the depths, regret overwhelms me. If the beast is not already awake, it will surely now rise. Into the empty mines, I run. Into nowhere and nothing.

Fleeing in shame and disgust. In fear. A most terrible trick. Now I have unleashed something awful upon the world. Now what lurks beneath, blinded by a life in the dark, will climb up and out. An albino terror, pale, translucent skin. Unblinking white eyes. A sickness in me. A horror so physical. I am pestilence. I am plague-bringer. I am the end. I have lost time. And I have lost— I fear I may be trapped in this mine. I think days have passed since I crashed the cart down into the deepness. I think now I am abandoned to rot here. Now this is my tomb. My wandering has ceased. No longer can I tell up from down, left from right. The darkness has me blinded. During those lost days I ran. Then I walked. And many chambers and halls I moved through. And several more shafts almost brought my penance to an abrupt halt. Teetering on the edge of one, I wondered if it would be better to fall, for I would not die, just fall forever, like in my dreams. That seemed peaceful. Then I thought of the giant maw of the beast, stirring in the depths, opening wide, swallowing. So I went on. But an eternity within that belly. An eternity of that void, out of God's love. How to live such a life. How to dwell within that cavernous creature's interior. To travel through this underworld, both a prisoner and a passenger within, taken deeper into the earth. A double blindness. Twice removed from God. Now here I brace myself against the black rock in some antechamber. Here I am waiting and listening. Here I am praying. There are no words written to use in his honour. He has never given to me any lamentations or hymns. For words are the embodiments of sins. Prayers are formless mutterings, sounds made to impersonate actual words. My intention, though, is clear. My meaning comes through in my tone and cadence. Normally my morning ritual is full of prayer, before my rounds of the Tower begin. Those hours are calm and measured. Now, cornered in this impossible dark, my breathing is panicked and hurried. The rhythm, inelegant. Forced. This will not do. And as my breath in ragged gasps slows, as I push myself back into the wall to gain control, I hear it. Hear it through my body. Through my bones. Rising from a hissing fizzle, like the sound of fire, but building in intensity. As the hissing becomes a rumble, moving through the rock walls behind, beneath, all around me. Me crying out. The creature. And yet the sound moves in warm waves, through the fabric of the cavern. As my body tenses in fear, expecting at any moment the explosion of rock and earth as the beast tears through, the undulations grow stronger, and a peace moves into my muscles. A great grinding. Not from below, from all around. A subsonic pulse that is not of this place yet seems to breathe through it, a carrier wave for something else. There are no words in the voice of God. It shivers through the rumbling of rock as a shifting fuzz of white, like the televisions we used to have. He is like interference. A broadcast coming through to me from far off, yet struggling to push through all this rock and ore and earth. This great subterranean lung. This throat. Body shivering, but not with cold or trepidation. A zealous, uncontrollable shaking as He speaks directly to me in the sublime language. Gasping and panting, the wet of my mouth moving in an ecstasy. Tasting the blood from my nose and gums. In my mouth. Truly this is what forgiveness feels like. From that burning sound, from within that shimmering noise, his message is clear to me. Climb the Tower. Look upon the face of God. Recover his light. The words are burning into my mind. I am rocking in place, nodding furiously. Yes. Yes. Yes. Climb the Tower. Yes. Look upon the face of God. Yes. Recover his light. Yes. This is now my quest. Finally my God has rewarded me for my commitment and duty. He has seen the fire fading in the Tower and will have me recover his holy beacon to bring warmth and life back. To bring back what was lost. I am forgiven. And those words repeat again and again. The voice of God hissing and crackling, for several hours, until I am sweat and blood and beaten muscle. Unable to walk, for the weakness in my legs. Hands over my face, smearing the blood and snot. The power of God is immense, and not intended for human comprehension. Most exposed to his word would die. Not since the Before have I heard his voice speak to me so directly. It is always there, but a low ebb. A throbbing of a sound, more within me than without. I always knew He was there, that He was watching. Always his presence. Always his invisible hand. An urgency now, as the strength returns to me. To leave this cavern and return to the Tower. To begin my ascent. And yet I am lost here. Still the darkness surrounds and enwombs me. There is a moment of worry. The shape of the sightless albino. But a breeze on my neck and I am standing. Moving towards the fresh air that beckons. Towards the surface. Long ago, deep in the darkest part of the mine, under a harsh fluorescent lamp, my pick shattered the black rock into a thousand sharp, gleaming pieces, revealing a perfectly round, silver ball. So dense. So heavy. And when I held it in my hands, God spoke to me in a voice so powerful I ran red with

blood and awoke in the Tower
infirmary after three weeks in a
coma. Running now through
the mine, so sure of my footing.
The passages and tunnels all
leading upwards, all pointing to
the sky now. And I am laughing.
I am crying. So happy, more
than I can remember being.
Here and there, a pause to
check, to close my eyes and feel.
It is inside me. The Tower. It
never leaves. I can sense its
location now, even in the dark
and underground. And as I
scramble up, there is light.
Though weak, the light of the
moon glimmers through clouds.
I know there is relief. And a
hissing kind of noise from the
light. My heart leaping, for God
is showing me with light and
his voice. Yet it is rain. The floor
here runs wet now, and I smell
that aroma of damp grass and

metal that always comes with showers. Down to grazed knees in the water pooling in the black rock, splashing my face, my body, inside my mouth. I am alive. I am connected with sky through this. I am cleansed. So moonlight flashes now in the puddles, picking up edges in silvery grey lines. My God revealed himself to me in the deep of the mine. He showed himself through the holy artefact I recovered there. That silver shape, a sphere so perfect it was unlike anything in nature. Only the hand of God could create something so pure and place it somewhere so far from human touch—and yet I found it. I was blessed. God reached out his mighty hand and touched me. He chose me. And only me. Now I emerge into the rain and the night, arms open to the sky. Mouth wide to feel the essence of the heavens run into and out of me. To pour down my body and wash away the dirt and filth of so many days crawling. To cleanse me before I ascend. And a hesitation now. A pause. A look over the shoulder to the great arch of stone and the world throat beyond. I am hunger. I am driven by my desire to go on. To climb as high as God himself. I must. So the darkness of those tunnels gives way to black mass of Tower. No blinking light. No sound to carry over the land. Just solid black with a backdrop of star-dabbled night. And beyond, the City. Another world. Another time. This well-worn path. How many feet have worked the ground over the years? How many of us took this route day after day, Tower to mine, mine to Tower? How many years, centuries? When groups of men took to the path, they had nothing to fear. Strong and dedicated, yet blind to the futility of their actions. Like me. Like I was. And now. That changed when I let them hear the voice of God. How far the ravage has coursed over the years since. How much of the rot and ruin spreads and grows. Moonlight is bright and the ground is veined in silvery sinews. And I will not touch. The smell of that wasteland is rank, makes me cough. And the silence goes on. And anxiety in the breathing, a slow and ragged rasp. Lungs ache from inhaling so much dead air, that damp mist drifting up from those glinting spindles. Slow motion movement, yet such urgency. Desperation. Clenching fists.

Unclenching. A twisted knot of stomach and grinding teeth. The ground slides beneath my feet in sluggish drags, and I am waist deep in an ocean of tar. In those dreams where I am trying to run but my legs are leaden. And something. And something is shaking in the scrubland. Amongst the black leaves of bushes leading down to a ditch. A shivering. A dog shaking off water. And the silence. Then that rustle. There is nothing before me but the night and the black bushes. There is nothing in me but the thundering of blood in my ears. Here, this fool moving closer to that wall of bush and grass, towards the darkness and within the sound. And only breath, heaving and fragmentary. The rush of blood in my ears. Something is beyond. And then my breath catches in my throat and silence. A yelp. Sharp and sudden from ahead. And I stagger backwards, hands outstretched. Again the noise, ringing out across the night towards me. And I turn my back to it, eyes closed, shaking head. No. No it cannot be that. It cannot. I sit in the earth, holding the weight of my head in these hands. The yelping, the plaintive ringing going on. I will not listen. I will not acknowledge trickery of this nature. There are faces flickering before me. Grey shapes and ghosts. And the possibility. The longing for. But none of that can be. And my mind going back to the mine. Back to the shaft and the tumbling metal cart. The roaring sound in my ears now the crash and cacophony of that falling. My body lurches, catching myself in the midst of a great drop into nothingness. I open my eyes. Here I stand now, and turning towards those bushes, hands pulling aside the black arms, moving through. And beyond here, a ditch. So down into the hollow, this shallow slope, piled high with so many wrecked metal hulks. The shattered glass. The shattered Before. The yelping, yelling ricochets from further down amongst the twisting and rusting. Inside the body of a large destroyed hull. Paint peeling in strips like the skin of an ancient beast. And flashes of something enormous and white and terrible. Here is the sound, within this rusted belly. I pause and look up, seeking out the Tower. I look up towards the highest point. I look up to God. Then tapping gently on the steel skin. Then a terrified knocking.

At once desperate to discover, and afraid of what will be revealed. Answered from within by a frantic sound, an animalistic floundering of noise and scraping. Backing away from this sudden flurry. Something lies trapped within this overturned shell. Some creature. Searching for an opening. And here a smashed window, partially pushed through. These hands, weak and useless as they are, force what remains and it falls to the inside of the hulk. And a thrashing, a crazed whimpering, and snuffling. A flurry of shadows. And so slipping through that ragged opening, heart racing. Here in the dark within, the shape of a small dog. It tries to leap at me, barking, but one of its rear legs is caught in a rent in the floor. It falls back and cries, and my heart fills with sorrow for the poor creature. So small and thin. So desperate. How long trapped here in the dark, I wonder? How long alone? I hush it quietly. Make calming sounds and reach a hand to it, as before with the dogs in the gardens. Such whimpering and sniffing. It appears uncertain whether to flee or reach for me. We each assess the other for a short time. The small brown nose sniffing my hand, my fingers touching its ears gently. And slowly it becomes calm. And gradually my heart slows. Here I move around the body of the dog. It follows my movements keenly as I examine its trapped leg. Its struggling has caused the metal to bite into its flesh. Dried blood crusts, and fresh red is leaking now. I run a hand over its body and hush. And my mother's hand in my hair. And my mother's calming laments. I pull the rusty flaps aside, twisting them until enough space is there for the dog to lift its leg free. And then we are in each other's arms. My face is wet and warm and full of the stench of its breath. Startled, alarmed for short moments, and then laughter as I embrace my new friend. Friend. A word I have not thought of for a very long time. I lift him up through the hole I entered through, and follow, pulling myself free of this metal hull, trashed and turned into the black earth. And there is no sign of the small dog. I call noises into the night. I bark like a dog barks. And I drop from the wreck into the ditch, peering in the darkness. And a snarling sound behind me. And the snatch of breath. Then the clamp of teeth into leg. All the noise in the world. All the noise in my body, pushing now through my mouth. Senseless screaming and wailing, a thrashing of arms, and a tumbling, falling, dragging over ground on my back. Hands grabbing to the grass, to the bushes, all sliding through. And further into dark. Further into ditch and dark. Another noise, snarling, roaring. Unlike anything I have ever heard. Guttural and raw, the sound of some creature in bloodlust. And I cannot believe I am betrayed. I cannot believe I am so easily fooled. And yet the animal urge to survive. It is in us all. And I can grasp the sides of the cold metal and hold. I can kick with my free leg until the solid something beneath my foot gets slick and wet and the biting loosens. That roaring, an angry raging, interrupted with a whimper of pain as my foot beats down. And it won't let go. And I am sure I am going to be consumed. Then another noise. Then a high pitched barking, angry and ferocious, but not of the thing that attacks me. It lets go as a torrent of raging animal sounds thrash in the darkness. And I reach out into the space of that creature with both hands. Finding those soft eyes and gouging and hearing the scream and feeling the roar in my chest and the slick blood in my hands. Running now, a blind staggering through this night. Towards the Tower. Towards safety. Leaving behind the rotted wasteland, the mine, and the thing that attacked me. And I am sure it pursues. I can hear its ravenous breath and snarling. See its albino bulk lurching through the darkness. This is what I surely awoke in those tunnels below ground. This is the price I pay now for my stupidity. My anger. And as I run, so too my leg runs red. The pain searing but cannot be allowed. Cannot stop me. But I grow weak. Pushing through it all. This body sweating. My vision beginning to grow blurry as I cross the rows of rusted shells, and the Tower looms up before me. Such a monolith. Some architectural wonder. And I rest against the body of the closest hulk, chipped and peeling blue from its outer skin, melted interior, all frozen dripping of plastic and rubber. My hand leaves a print of deep red against its side. As the ancients. Staggering to the smashed doors that will be safety. Will be home. Already the heat of the fire, and the orange glow warms my body. Already I am smiling as I drag my wounded leg over the floor of the hall, and pass out with the flames casting long shadows over my beaten— Body. Waking in alarm. To wet, sniffing, nuzzling into this face. Urgent whining. And for a moment I have been tracked. Followed. Hunted. Here I am to be eaten alive by the giant mouth of that terrible creature of the dark— And yet there is no biting. There are no teeth ripping. And when light breaks these eyelids, the large brown eyes of a dog before me. It pushes into full vision, the eagerness of youth as tongue lolls and laps, snout warm and damp. Momentarily the dog is pushed away, into the shadows cast by the orange of the huge dying fire. But it barks playfully and looks at me with friendly eyes. And here a torn ear. Bloody fur. And so it was this small animal that came to my aid. This was the barking and yelping in the dark as I lay torn. And now I am both confused and immensely grateful. I live now because it came to me. I have always been aware of the wild dogs that roam the lands around the Tower. Normally shy and nervous of my shape. It is unusual for one to stray close to the Tower. More so to enter. I reach my hand out, welcoming. It approaches, an eagerness and excited panting. A smile for my new friend. Soft fur and warm. There were dogs in the Before. In the Tower. They were walked and played in the grand central gardens. These wild ones must be the descendants of those. Running fingers over this one's head. What legacy of this. Now this wounded leg. Now the bloody mess around the bite. That red is sticky, drying in the heat. How long was I unconscious? Could have been hours, maybe only minutes. The bite is ragged and oozes thick red. It will need cleaned and dressed. So standing, and my new companion barking and leaping. Yes, come. Outstretched hand to show, to follow. To climb these stairs while injured will challenge, will bring pain. Yet reach my apartment. Yes. To rest there until fit. Yes. Then to climb. Then to ascend. Dog is running ahead, leaping stairs and turning, expectant looks. Then off ahead again. It brings a feeling long forgotten, unfelt for many years. A joy. A simple joy in another creature to share time. The Tower has been for so long a source of extremes, and now. But what if my God grows jealous? For He and I have long been united, long been tied together in this existence and struggle. We are the Tower. Might He view Dog as a distraction from my quest? And yet, Dog was given to me by the good grace of God. Yes. He is kind and generous, truly. I should not doubt. His plan is unknowable by the likes of me. Dog runs into and out of the various rooms and corridors, exploring all the Tower we pass. He returns with odd bits and pieces in his mouth, which he drops at my feet. Runs off. Lumps of plastic, melted and twisted, children's toys, and unidentifiable blackened objects. And the Before, people down in the gardens throwing balls for their pet dogs, games of fetch. I stop and stare down at the burning gardens, looking for the running and dashing of dogs, the calling out of people. Now only the glowing orange of flame. And so I stoop to pick up the twisted objects Dog has dropped at my feet. They are cast into the fire, as is my duty. To burn all that was before. To erase that life and that world. The Tower must be stripped clean. Then a pause. Standing with some mangled lump of plastic in my hands, and Dog looks at me with his brown eyes. His tongue panting. Expectant. I toss the object down the corridor, and a smile crosses my face as he dashes after it. Skidding feet and legs across the floor. He returns to me, carefully placing his new toy at my feet. And he sits there looking at it. So we play there, out on the landings, in the hallways, as we move up through the floors of the Tower. Slow limping. Sleek skidding. And my hand reaches to his head each time. He leaps to me and licks my face. I hold his small body. Now the fourth floor, and the toy bounces down the hall and through a doorway into an apartment. I open my mouth to call out to Dog, to not go in there, but he is gone already, disappearing into that darkness. I recognise this hole. There is a mark on the wall, a black X I drew myself. I have never been inside. Not since— I never go inside. And barking of Dog. And leaking of red. The pain coursing now. Hand clamped to the bite marks, slick with my body. And barking of

Dog. I do not go in that apartment. Never go in that apartment. I call wordlessly to Dog. Standing in the hall, the doorway before me, like an archway, beginning to loom in my vision. Something beginning to shudder. Dog's barking coming to me. But only his barking. He does not emerge. His urgency. Loud and insistent. He appears in that doorway, turns and runs back inside. He is clear. He is leading now. And it occurs to me that perhaps he is a guide, sent to show me the way. So I have no choice. I must follow. And it fills my chest with a cloying. My throat tightening. I hold up my shaking hands and clench them into fists, and they shake all the more intensely. And so into the-place-I-do-not-enter. The rooms that have been a blind spot these years. Blurred out of vision. Unacknowledged. I would have buried this apartment if I could. I would have burned it all. Tore it from the Tower and cast it into the sun. And now I am dragging my bleeding body inside. This dark room. The shapes of furniture. Armchairs and bookcases. I know the books on those shelves well. Beyond there is a single bedroom and a bathroom. A small kitchenette. The smell of fresh cooking. Clean laundry drying. I used to know the person who lived here. I knew her name. I knew the shape of her face and would listen to the sound of her voice for hours. But she is not here. No more. This place is empty. Her absence. There is the mirror above the couch, faded and spotted now from the smoke and the dust and ash. The couch we sat on. And I do not want to move any closer. The threshold is as far as I can go, as far as I should have. To go further would be to open it all. And no. Not now, not after all this time. Dog's bark from the bedroom. And my bleeding leg. So I limp to him. Over carpet familiar in pattern. And I push the door. Here an empty bedroom I know too well. Here a bed, unmade from the last morning she rose. And if I were to lie on that bed, her scent would fill my lungs and all this would end. Consumed by a darkness that would put out all the light. This is nothing now. This is a shadow. The inverse of a living space. This hand to the door handle and clenching it and slamming the door closed. Swallowing down the lump.

Pushing it out. A hand wipes blood across my face. And the barking, scratching of claws from the other side. For a long moment, standing. Staring at the faded white paint on the door. The wood grain. The brush strokes. The door open a crack, enough for him to escape and bound through the room. He is oblivious. To be so free. Here on this couch, bleeding. Here is the seat of rejection and shame. Now my leg shedding blood on the surface soaked with tears, so many. And these hands working to strip these discarded clothing items, to tie the tourniquet. To stem the flow. And Dog, comfortable and content there, lying, head and paws towards the floor. To be angry with him would be cruel. He was not to know. Could not have known. And yet, from God he is sent, and so. Why does He bring me here, after all this time? Despite it all, there is a sense of wellness in these rooms. Sinking into the worn upholstery—the breathing of Dog, his small body rising and falling. His calmness. His warmth. This leg is burning pain and blood, yet there is sleep coming. And I am unable to resist. I loved her. But she would not believe. Until the day I brought her the holy artefact. And this apartment was never opened again. Until— The people from Before. Most are faces and voices. Some names. Many are lost. Here in the Tower, their memories are columns of smoke that rise on the updrafts from the fire, condense and return to the earth as black ash rain. Her memory remained locked in here. In that bedroom. Her memory cannot be allowed to escape into the air. It cannot rain down to the ground and churn and twist into the dirt, down into the deep. No release. A dreamless sleep. When these eyes are open, Dog appears and seems to smile. A lick of the face and two paws on the shoulders. My hands hold his thin body, feeling the bones of his ribs. His heart beating. He wants to stay here. This homely apartment is comfortable, safe. But this is not for living. Only decay and rot here. And so standing already, pushing from the couch, leg stiff but bleeding has slowed. There were once crutches and walking frames in the Tower hospital. Now the fire has consumed them. Dog sprawls on the couch, a yawn splitting his snout. His eyes follow me to the doorway, watch me stand and walk out. He barks. Dog is staying. The time for this place has gone, and the way is out. There is reluctance in his walk to the door. But there is nothing in there for us. The door is closed, and we move on. The hissing of water into fire signals the arrival of rain. On the fifth floor, a pause by the railing to look upon the gardens below. Once a lush green escape from the work of the Tower. Fountains and streams, the laughter of children. The families together. The men playing boules to distract them from the hard days spent in the mine. The song of birds. And the days we spent, together. In hands. Turning away. Fire can obliterate all but memory. To be blackened of heart. To be scorched of mind. Why can God not make me forget? Because penance. Because duty. Because sin is forever. Water running down from the floors above. That constant trickle. Dog pauses to lap at a dirty puddle. This mouth is open to God. Inside the sprawl of my apartment, Dog finds a spot to curl into. He watches, silently. His company is welcome, and these rooms seem to breathe like they have not before. And in my room, amongst the bedding and detritus, I am hiding. Within the coil of my nest I curl and twist, teeth set as that stinging pain in my chest gives vent. I am just bees. I am buzzing tears. I cannot change what has gone before, but somehow I must purge it. I must erase the history, the memory. And God has given me the chance. All that has been done must be undone. And I am gasping breath. I am ragged, torn wheezing as my hands grapple for my body to hold myself. And then the warm nose, the gentle face. The shuffling beside me. And Dog is there, his brown eyes meeting mine. His black nose touches my face. And we are together. And everything will be okay. He stays with me for hours. And I am planning the ascent. Counting the floors. Recalling the obstacles. There have been some collapses. Fire damage and— There is a long way to go. A long journey. Some apartments are familiar. Time has been spent in them before. Yet none are like the other. There is at least that. How long will it take? How many days? I do not know. Never before have I undertaken such a task. Never have I dared to venture so high, and in such a time. I have wandered far and over all these floors, but over the many years, and languishing here and there. Now I am to climb with purpose. With my injured leg. Although I grow stronger, and God will guide me, I hesitate. I stand on the brink of eternity now. There are no other people. It will be a lonely ascent, but Dog will ease that. Many of the higher floors I have not been to for many years. I am unsure what to expect. And thoughts of a weapon. Of defence. But surely there is nothing here that can harm me now? Not within sight of God. He will protect me during this journey, shield me from serious harm. Difficulty awaits for certain. He does not want this to be an easy task. Yet I am sure that I will be saved from harm and welcomed into his presence to receive his ultimate blessing, and return with his divine light. When we leave, there are shafts of bright day cutting across the throat of the Tower. Motes of dust and the rising column of fading smoke shimmer through golden rays. A scene as beautiful as the mystery that is God. This Tower. And as we rise, my feet on the stone stairs, Dog by my side, it is as though the Tower is opening up to me. All these years I have lived here. All the life I have given up to it. And yet how unknowable it has remained. Impenetrable. As implacable as the black rock from which it was carved. Now something is shifting. I feel a change. It is as though I could reach out and, instead of cold hard rock, my hand would sink into the soft, porous body of sponge. All these years this massif has absorbed, taken in all that I am. Now it breathes out. Exhales. This world lung. Even Dog appears to sense a shift. It was often said of dogs that they were aware of things most people were not. He stays close, no longer running off and exploring the various doorways we pass. Looming shadows and dark. Rising several floors, I am eager to make progress before nightfall when travelling through these higher hallways will become too dangerous. Along the way we stop here and there to pause. To rest. To cast these lumps and abandoned items of the Tower into the fire. Yet when I see Dog watching, expectantly, I allow a few minutes of play to pass. He runs and scampers, chasing his temporary toys through the halls. And I feel no panic as he slides into nearby apartments, for nowhere is like that other place. He can explore and be free. For a time. Eventually everything must burn. We continue our climb with wary eyes, for the floors here in places are damaged. There are gaps through which we might fall, and several stairwells are blocked by rubble. Which presents a problem. Here the rainwater from above flows over the edge of the overhang, cascading into the central gardens. A vision of something from another place. From picture books I have seen. That I remember, in my mother's arms, her stories whispered in the fading light of evening. Of adventure and exploration. Myth. I was a knight slaying great beasts in those dreams.

Now those pages are burned away. Now they are ash, as my dreams—seared to blackened char. Here we stop and the water runs dirty red and brown as I rinse myself. Clean my wound. Stronger now. Fresh and invigorated. This may be the best spot to rest now. To push my leg too hard at this point would be folly. And Dog appears to agree, stalking into a nearby apartment, tail wagging. This room is stripped bare. Through here I have been, many times, collecting and casting all into the fire. So against the wall, slumped, with Dog close by. This leg stretched straight, dressing checked, adjusted. Often I have attempted to work out how many apartments are in this Tower. How many families. How many lives. But I cannot be certain how many floors there are. Staring up to the higher floors from these lower areas, all that can be seen is the grey of a damp mist, smog created by the collecting moisture and smoke of the fire, rising up. From outside the Tower, the peak disappears into the sky, obscured by dark foggy cloud. I have often thought I could see something flashing within. And so those who lived here. Who moved within the walls of these rooms. Slept and ate here. Loved and argued. Lived and— There are stains on the walls. The white paint peels in strips. Large brown blemishes from leaking water and dirt in the pipes. The blood of the Tower. And also blackening from fire. From burning. That holy artefact came to the surface with my unconscious body. And when I awoke in the infirmary, that perfect sphere was still clasped in my hands. The doctors had been unable to prize it free, so tightly were my muscles seized. It was my calling then to share God's voice, to bring it to all the people of the Tower. And it was too overwhelming. For some it burned too bright inside them. Now unwanted faces. Now other voices, not of my God, pushing and demanding to be heard. All I want is sleep. All I need is rest and to continue to the top of the Tower. Then all those others will move on and leave me. And yet her face looms out of the many. Out of the mass of sound in my ears, her singular voice. And I cannot look. Cannot see. I do not want to hear it. Not again. Not now. This night passes in long periods of silence. Of stillness, intercut with the static of rain. Then frantic thrashing and noise. Then screaming. Then raging. I sometimes laugh. Flat on my back in this room, the ceiling moves around me. These walls throb to the beat of a heart unseen. Awkward shadows. The lurch of my body caught in columns of moonlight. And that sound. With my face to the floor, breathing in the dust, a great flapping of wings. A great movement of air. And when my eyes open. Here I stand beneath this waterfall, this cascade of rain. This water may be ancient. How high the Tower? How old the water? Like the journey of a great river, from mountains to ocean. Perhaps this is merely the cataract of this mighty black cliff. So the night washes away, like blood disappearing in water. Dog sniffs around me nervously. Tail down. I pat his head. He eyes me for a long moment. Uncertain. And I wonder now how much I can trust this animal that follows me. This wild creature from outside the Tower. From out of the sight of God. And yet we are bonded now. Yes. We two are as one. Men in the mine would often talk of their own animals, their companion dogs. Their need to discipline the animals, to train them, make them submit. This dog runs free by my side. Stays by my side through choice. And often tales of spirit animals in my mother's story books. Of men and women who can change. Transform. I look at this dog and wonder who he used to be. But those eyes are unknowable, and suddenly he barks. Tongue panting now. Yes. It is time to move on. It is dawn. There is sun beyond the apartment windows, rising sluggishly over the hill of the mine. Standing there in that glassless frame, the ground so far below. Thoughts of jumping have come before, but not now. And the mine there, deep down inside the hill. Inside the earth. Such churning. And what lurks in those depths? Now the rumbling of the Tower. Dog barks again, sharp and urgent. I step away from the window and together we are leaving behind these rooms. Together we are leaving behind this floor and climbing. We are going up. This is the next day. Here Dog seems more relaxed. He is wary of straying too far from me, and the rumbling of the Tower continues for some hours. Each throb, each pulse of movement, he turns. He barks.

These stretches of stone I am used to. There are no surprises in the movement of the Tower. God flexes, opens his throat, and all the light pours out. I wonder now why the Tower roars. Why, as I begin my ascent, it bellows and shakes. Perhaps the trumpeting of God's choir, announcing my intention to take up the challenge, to rise to the level of the immaculate. For otherwise, to think of anger, or rage. I could be mistaken. I could be trespassing into his realm, a place so high I have never dared venture. Someplace forbidden. But the voice of God was clear. The instructions absolute. I am unlike those others who could never hear it, or interpret it correctly. Some of them tried to transcribe what they heard. They sat shivering, clothes stuck to their sweaty bodies, as their hands moved over pages and pages of yellowed paper, scrawling wild, uncontrollable language. The fools. The voice of God is more than words. Beyond language. All they did was hasten their own downfall. It was then it became clear that words and books were sinful. That all language, all attempts to transcribe holy communication, should be banished forever. And so cast into those flames. At these heights of the Tower, it was once possible to smell the burning of paper, plastic, rubber, wood—the melting of metals. The fire burned with such intensity in those days, it was choking. For a time it was necessary to wrap the face in rags, as we did in the mines. Stalking the Tower with goggles and mask, through the belching fog of black smoke rising in a thick churning column up the centre. And my arms raised to Heaven. This hallway, from stairwell to the central open corridor over the gardens. The crash of the great internal waterfall. And Dog barks, running, disappearing around the corner. Limping after. In through this doorway, into the cavernous apartment, lying wrecked and abandoned. All the others. I know this place. Unlike that other marked series of rooms, this apartment I do return to. This is no knot of memory that fails to untie and become forgotten. This is no place of shame. This is where I grew up. Within these walls I lived as child. My hand now to the blackened plaster. A light touch. A faint smile. Dog emerges from what were the bedrooms, panting happily. I nod, and he finds a corner to curl into. I am unsure why he has guided me to this place. If sent to me by God, then it seems strange to return to these sources of pain and sadness, guilt and lost happiness. Perhaps this is all a punishment. My hand slides down the wall, the roughness of the surface blossoming like sparkling neon lights. This was one of the last apartments to be cleared out. I resisted for years, but eventually I submitted to the flames. To my God. All that once was, all that was my childhood, fell into fire. It was liberating. For a time. To be freed of that past. Only now— Along this wall my mother's bookcase was placed, stacked full of stories, bound in soft and hard covers, alive with words and imagery that aroused my imagination. How brightly they all burned. Such conflicted feelings. And why I return here over and over. To sort through those thoughts, to process my feelings—meditate on what God expects of me. And yet, this is the only set of rooms in the entire Tower where his voice does not reach me. Within these walls there is silence. Sometimes that is truly why I come here. For a few hours. And I come here when my faith is in doubt. When on the verge of abandoning my God. And I am reminded of all that came Before, and the lessons, stories, values my mother taught me. So when I return to his voice, it is with a renewed conviction. I reach God through my mother's words. Here I allow my hand to move along the wall, leading me deeper into the rooms, back to the darker places. Where I slept as a child. This small box room now. Once a bed against that wall. Once a curtained window, now blasted and exposed to the elements. And once a child crouched at that window, entranced by the many lights in the sky. And those of the City. That mystery. That magic. How I dreamed of the cold light of those streets. The sounds of life moving at such speeds. Faster than my eyes could see. It was a place people went to and were changed by it, my mother said. Sometimes they returned, and were not the same as when they left. And when I lay in my bed, warm and secure, my mother's voice reading to me until I slept, and sunk into an ocean of words. Of princes and princesses, dragons and mythical beasts, epic quests through dangerous lands. But her failing eyes. Her failing husband. My father. I look now to these walls, my childhood shelter from— Such a useless man. And yet, in his shadow I walk. In his footsteps, down into the mine to work. But not like him. Nothing like him. Never. A promise made to an angry youth in a mirror, fists bloody, eyes red. The sound of my mother weeping alone. I slump down the wall, crouching here in the dark, these eyes closing and my face becoming wet. Those slurred words now. Violent and raging. Bestial sounds made by an inhuman mouth. Roaring through the apartment halls. And me hiding beneath my covers, terrified. And him, out there, lying in the living room, sprawled on the floor or the furniture, drunk and incapable. A man alone shouting out into the darkness. Close my eyes tight. Clench my fists. Curl into the corner. Sometimes she would come to my room and hold me. Together we would hide from him. Together seeking refuge from the dragon he became. Other times he would hear her, catch sight of her shadow moving, and launch vileness at her. Clamber over the furniture towards her— And those moments I do not want to recall or hear again. Returning now to what was the living room, for a moment the image of how it once was flashes before me. There the armchair my mother sat in, where she sometimes read to me as I sat on the floor. And there the couch he lay slumped on. Where he snored and moaned like a bloated white beast. Where he swore and commanded. I crouch in the corner by Dog and he leans into me. I pat his head gently. I think of my mother's calming voice. I think of her words like a gentle flow of water. And I sleep. So unlike the voice of my God. My mother spoke honey and gossamer. She spoke words so soft and without edges, each one blending into the next. A river of language. Of images and stories. For me her voice was always sleep. Dream. Comfort. It was safety and solitude. Next to her, in her arms, and embrace. The only place I ever felt safe. Except for— My God speaks to me in a language so complex and wordless. So unnatural. And where my mother's voice brought contentment and calmness, most who heard the voice of God found themselves unable to contain it, and were marked with sickness. Gradually the hospital began filling with them, and then more rapidly, as more and more heard him calling. We looked for the source of the plague in the water and sewerage system. In the food. We even searched the mine. And as the disease spread and people began to fall, I asked God to bring them a cure. My eyes open here, slumped against the wall, a sweating collapsed shell of a man. Here is a waste of skin. There is rain falling outside the Tower. There is quiet in the rest of the apartment. Dog stirs beside me. Opens his mouth to yawn. To look upon the face of God is no easy task. I, and I alone, can hear and bear the immense weight of the voice. To

hold a vision of God in my eyes would surely burn any other man to ash. And as my mother's eyesight deteriorated more over the years, so her voice grew more sonorous, more poetic. Unable to read the stories from her many books, she instead turned to spinning tales of her own. Blurring the lines between our own lives and the magic of those myths she read to me all the years before. Now there were trolls down in the mines. There were fairies amongst the plants and trees of the gardens. The twinkling of starlight, the gleam of the City, was a glitterfall of stardust over our world. And when my father's lumbering, his booming voice —
then I knew the dragons were real. Now this shuddering in the walls. The movement in the Tower increasing. And Dog

startled. So this hand goes to calm him. And yet the rumbling, heaving of walls is more. There is a lurching, a sudden shift, and Dog yelps, disappears into the dark. Me tumbling as the room spins, and a great crack. Air fills with the choking fog of dust. There is nothing to hold. There are no hands to reach out to me. And then nothing. And then the silence. Here I am flat. There is the whimpering approach of Dog. We each look at the other. We each know the Tower has moved. The angles are different. The floor no longer level. It is as if a huge shifting of the very earth has occurred. Only God can make the earth shudder in such mighty movements. Only He would see fit to open the ground, split open the skin of the world so that all that is below is exposed.

The fiery. The undulating red and orange. My God has a plan. A reshaping. A new mould for the world. He seeks to change the structure of all things, the grand architect. And as He remakes the world, He remakes me. There is the sense of it growing within. The suggestion of a new mode of being. My Ascent. My becoming. What a glorious transformation must be awaiting. An immaculate purging, to render me clean of all sin and rot. These things must be leached from within me. Must be pulled out, brought to the surface, revealed to the light of God. And I know, can feel it within me, pushing up out of the darkest, deepest parts of my being. Something inside is rising up. And I fall into a corner of the room and vomit. And I am laughing as that filth splatters against walls and floor. Such a stink. I roll backwards, push myself away from the mess. That reek pooling out towards me, wanting to rejoin. I lie flat on my back, within the shuddering room, this floor at all angles. He has reached out and touched me. Even here, within this isolated space. Then as I feel Dog nuzzling, his hot snout pushing against my face, the soft murmur of my mother's voice. And now, perhaps I realise that it is she who wishes me remade. It is she who asks me to give up what has stained my soul black. My tears. And I wonder if I could be wrong. My faith, all my hopes, misplaced. It is possible my God is not be the one guiding me. Instead my mother—ever watchful, ever loving. And Dog whines as his wet nose pushes against me. I stare at those brown eyes and wonder what spirit occupies this small animal. Sitting up and this hand going and moving over his lithe body. Those eyes looking up, so deep and unknown. I believed him sent to me by God, to show me the way, and yet to this apartment he has brought me. Back to my mother. I try to move my mouth in that shape. I try to ask the question, but only those empty breaths. And the thought, the question that spins my head, makes me so dizzy I lurch suddenly to one side as if the Tower were once again shaking. A long groan pushes up out from my lungs as I ponder the true face of God. So there is only one way to go. Only one decision now. Up. Onwards. To continue rising through the Tower, so that I might stand in the presence of my God and ask. So that I might see for myself, once and for all. Now the windows are skewed. The room is off balance. As strength returns to these legs and standing leaning awkwardly against slanted walls. Beyond these window frames, and into the drowning sun evening. I face an uncertainty never known. This Tower has always been solid. The future always seemed set. It is all changing. Outside the apartment, shambling gait and Dog. This view now is altered. Unfamiliar. There are collapses. Sections of corridor above have fallen. Down below, in the gardens, there lies debris of all kinds, and the fire glows hot and angry. An energy that fills me from within. I feel my sweat. I feel my moment. Progress for these next floors is swift. No time is wasted. No diversions. Such is the urgency and intensity to move on and progress. To reach higher. And Dog, his tail wagging and his barking, spurring my pace. Not since the mines has this body moved so. Years since these muscles ached, and the pain was good. This sweat real and the heaviness in my chest. Climbing, each stairwell succumbing, though the awkward sloping. Soon I can feel the main floor of the Tower, the heart of the community. This is where people came to meet, to buy their food and clothing. This was the place of entertainment and social life. This was where those not in the mines worked. This was the school. The hospital. This was the place all Tower life came to be. Here there is the Tower hub.

Here is where people gathered to enjoy fountains and music. And now all is still. No chattering of conversation, or the laughter. No lull of strings. Instead the wrecked plaza. The smashed windows and toppled planters, once blossoming trees and flowers and bushes. The scorched ground. And standing under what was once a great skylight, only desolation here now. All emptiness and abandonment. This had been the busiest area of the Tower before. And after, it was my busiest area. So much to erase. So much to cast down into the fire. It took many long months. Still sometimes I come through these streets, high up in the Tower, patrolling, searching. Many times things are missed. Much remains hidden. Yet the last few times there was nothing.

Just the wreckage of all that went before. It is late. So late it is early. The sun will be pushing over the hill of the mine. I must rest. This leg aches and the body shudders with the effort of this climb. But the sense of achievement is great. What progress has been made. And so now through the main street, and the stores that line both sides. This was where my mother brought me, for school books and clothes, for visits to the doctor when I was sick, for birthdays and days amongst people, enjoying cakes and music. All of this now forbidden by God. And the contrast. The conflict within. This growing sense of unease. The questions that have so long been buried in the dark. A crack of light. But I cannot allow myself to become distracted. This doubt. My questioning faith. This could all still be a test. So I move here through these wrecked stores, all empty and broken. And yet the breaking was not mine. The shuddering Tower has caused much damage these years. Without proper care, things fall apart. They decay. The stripping walls of apartments, the cracking floors, the broken plaster, concrete, glass. For a while it was as though the very rock were tearing itself apart. An attempt to return to the earth. All this commerce. All these words and music. The heart of the Tower and the heart of its sin. How ignorant we all were. The lives we led, far from God's grace. We didn't know. We were arrogant. And here I work to pay for those sins, so that we may all find peace. So we may all be forgiven. I did what was required in God's name. Did I not? This street loops back to the plaza, and the dawn is pouring in through the skylight. Beyond is the hospital. Where, in the darkness of my own mind, I understood God's message and intention, and awoke. To the edge of the plaza, the metal railing that runs its length overlooking the gardens. The cold metal, damp to these hands. Now across this yawning chasm, the Tower's interior, I see the rows and rows of empty apartments, black holes staring back at me from the distant gloom. Early morning light is beginning to rise up the opposite side, revealing the administrative section of the plaza. This mezzanine level curves around to that side, a walkway of trees and fountains overlooking the gardens far below. Over there is where the mine work was controlled. Rooms full of maps and charts, men studying geological studies. Sciences of the deep earth. Now those rooms just rumble with their emptiness. The Tower shakes them. Mocks them. I look around here for Dog, and catch sight of him skulking along the walkway. His small brown body moves amongst the wreckage. Then he pauses and sits. Eyes seem to seek me out. As a youth, a brash, arrogant child, I argued with my mother on that promenade. She wept and pleaded with me. And I turned my back on her. Her eyesight had almost completely failed her by then. A year later and she was dead. And alone in the world, I joined the other men—my father— down in the depths of the mine.

And so began my journey out of sin. So again I look at Dog sitting there, and he looks back at me. And again I wonder. I flush as I recall those things I shouted on that day. My embarrassment now. My shame. What hurt I caused. Never apologised for. Never amended. Never forgiven. I am on a path of absolution. Atonement. And this small dog leads the way. I cannot continue meeting his gaze. Here I look away, as the voice of God begins to thunder through my body. I raise my face to the heights of the Tower, to where the eyes of God look down upon me. From where his mighty voice booms. That unseen summit. The unknowable peak. My goal. It is somewhere I have never been. It strikes me now, standing here, that I have never been as high as

I now aim to climb. Never have I known those far reaches of the Tower. In the Before, they were simply off limits—a constant construction site, full of engineers and architects, the intellectuals of our home. After, when the sounds of the Tower fell into silence, those floors became the realm of God, a place beyond my comprehension and where I had no right to set foot. So dirty and unclean as I am. But I am invited now. I am beckoned—no, I am guided. Here this dog, this animal sent to me to lead me higher and higher, and I feel now something inside me shifting. Is this dog a ghost from my mother, or a messenger of my God? Moving now over to the mezzanine walkway, to join Dog there and sit with him. He pants close to my face and I feel warm. My arm goes around his body. The view down from here, dizzying if you are not used to it. As children we played here sometimes, when parents were not watching so closely. We chased each other around these pathways, we dared each other to look down for as long as we could. We tried to spot our own homes from this great height. And down at the very bottom, the gardens, full of sport and games and people taking in the greenery. Now a smouldering orange blur, ashen grey spreading around all that the fire has touched, consumed, spat out. Once, sitting here alone, I could feel the rising heat from those flames. I sat here and felt that energy move over me, a vibrant wind—God's breath—climbing up through this chimney, this throat, to the forbidden high floors above. And my neck cranes back to stare up. All that darkness. All that gathered smoke and ash and fog. An impenetrable cloud awaits me. What will I discover within? A growl now—but not from dog. From within. From the Tower. The rock itself. Some rumbling from far below, and a violent shaking vibrating its way up the fabric of the building. Through me. Bone-shuddering. And I look up to God, and out of the gathered fog and cloud of dust, a twisting shape. What face is forming within that umbra? The churning, coiling shadow and soot, moving together in the shape of a creature. Something becoming in the heights. Something emerging from the blackness. And I see that beast. The terror of the dark underworld. That thing that has haunted my memories and dreams, my time spent in penance in the mine. Here now, gathering itself into some ashen mass, ready to descent upon me, to swallow me whole into it's huge belly. To be blind within that cavernous stomach. And as the Tower continues to shudder, and to lurch now, so I run. Here I drag myself back towards the main plaza area. I am sweat and meaningless noises falling from this mouth. I see it in my mind. I see that dragon flexing muscles, wings, talons, all black as char. Then that carapace cracks and shatters into fine dust, revealing its pristine white skin. It's dead grey eyes. Dog remains sitting on the walkway, panting. He stares after me and I shout out. He is oblivious, but he runs to my side. Together we make for the hospital and through the empty corridors and wards, the place I spent weeks in coma. Within this place we will be hidden from that creature. We will be safe from all that shuddering and shaking. And yet these white walls and floors make me pause and question. The pale white beast, and this cavern of alabaster tones. Then a room I recall. This room is a pool of darkness, so strong it is as if it glows with a black light. This room is a charred cell. Here something released immense energy that blasted the walls, floors, ceiling. Here the voice of God. I am not sure how to feel about this place now. This room. My home for some time during and after my coma. I look around for Dog and he is already sniffing around inside that sinkhole of a space. Have I once again been led? Without realising it, has my path been laid out for me? My hands move over the walls as I step through the shattered doorway. The cold cinders break and crumble through my fingers, and as ash float to the floor. Is this the state of my own mind now? A once solid wall now burned and broken, beginning to crumble under doubt. I am sick. Contaminated. So wretched and forsaken. Here crouching and now kneeling, wanting to cry, to push all my fears, my questions out, but not finding the movement. So much noise now, it pushes out the sound of my God. And all the trials to reach this point. This is when thoughts of turning back. Of going home. Of leaping into the sky and ending it all. This useless existence. I could find a window and jump. I could walk out to the plaza and let the great maw of that dragon consume me. Anything to make this stop now. To end this collapse of faith. Here are angles of a man across a filthy, scorched floor. Here are arms and legs outstretched. Here is giving up. Such is my dismay. And how alone I am here. Even Dog has left me. And what feels like hours. In this darkness, lying here on my back. Afraid. Hiding. And where is Dog? Now worry. Now concern. Unfamiliar feelings, so long since I felt anything like this, since I needed to care about anyone or anything besides myself. Now this small animal is all I have. My companion. Friend. What if he has got lost? Or fallen somewhere out amongst that rubble and collapse, with that albino creature looming and swooping, bringing so much thunder. On my feet and yelling pointlessly into the hospital hallways. My wordless voice reverberates off of the mouldy green walls. Dragging this body back the way I came. Forgetting now if he came with me. Did I leave him out there on the plaza? Hesitation now. Standing fitfully by this door. To run out and call to him. I cannot lose him. Cannot lose— And yet I am so scared. So overcome with— All this shame. Here I sit against the wall and wait. And this metal frame of a bed, once my place of recovery, so ragged and rusted. This was where gentle hands upon my brow, and my eyes snapped open. Standing now and out into the hallway. Out to find my friend.

Calling into each room. Down all the corridors. Out into the plaza, the Tower shaft empty. Empty of any monstrous white beast. I move slowly. Searching out in the heights, up into the smoke and fog that obscures God. Down to the far below floors, the gardens. Nothing seems hiding. Nothing but all this wreckage. My life in ruinous waste, all disintegrating into fire and ash. I shout down into those gardens far below. So far away no one could possibly hear. To the other floors. The balconies. My throat tastes blood, and the Tower echoes. Nothing moves. Nothing makes a sound but me and my mouth noise coming back to me as it spins from all the walls of the Tower. So I search the mall. Into the rows of stores, these streets. Yelling and shrieking. All these places empty and wrecked. And my chest aching. My throat burning. This is panic. Why would God give me a companion and then take him away? Is this a punishment for doubting him? Here I drop to my knees, hands clenched and praying, pleading. My moment of weakness. My elegiac pause. Please do not abandon me for my human faults and frailties. These I must overcome. Through your grace and guidance, I shall rise. Abandoned by my people. By my love. My companion and friend. Please, my God, do not leave me also. You have been the one true constant in my life. The singular point that gave me meaning. Purpose. Without God, there is no purpose. There is only rot and decay. Things that lead to sin and debasement. These things I have pledged to eradicate. To cleanse myself and my world of. Long minutes pass. The silence and my heavy breathing. And my tears that are shed for my friend, my animal companion, now lost. An innocent. The guilt. Leaking from me now and dripping, dropping from the tip of my nose to the ground on which I beg my God to forgive me. And now the Tower shaking again. Now the ground beneath me moving. The whole plaza shuddering. For a moment, standing, caught in alarm, just staring with eyes wide as the ground begins to crack. A long fissure along the whole section of the floor. The plaza is collapsing. Falling away and crumbling. A thundering quake rampages through. The structure. A wave of energy distorting the shape of everything. I see it ripple the ground before me. And my feet move. My legs spasm into action and I run and tumble and fall into the back of the mall, away from the overhanging plaza. Then a terrible crash, preceded by a great yawning noise. Such violent movement. I am slammed into the walls, into the floor. The noise goes on and on. The thunderous raging. And I know more floors below have been decimated by the rain of stone and steel. Face down in the dust and debris, I feel the shuddering stop, yet when I take my hands from my ears I can still hear the crashing and screaming of Tower. And yet the screaming might be me. And the crashing might be the raging in my own skull. No movement for so long. I cannot be sure if it is safe to move. Here the air is full of choking dust, falling all around, a deluge of destruction. And these eyes open. And there is no plaza. A vast chasm has appeared. As though something massive tore a section of the Tower with enormous hands. And my mind flashes. The albino beast. I drag myself as close as I dare to the edge, to where I stood moments before. Great areas of floor exposed by the collapse, the guts of the building. The wires and pipes and steel support exposed like veins, viscera, bones. Such a jagged mess. The creature is on the hunt. I am pursued by those claws and teeth. That mouth. Here it has taken a bite from the building. And down where all this ruin fell. Down in the gardens, where the fire burns—now there is blackness. Now there is an enormous hole, a great maw into the abyss. The mouth of the deep has opened up in God's Tower. Long have I felt the hands of darkness reaching out from the below, hands in the night that want to snatch and tear, drag me back down into that hollow. Sensed the presence of it. The shape of it growing down in the mines. What form that darkness takes now. What appearance. Something huge and terrible surely now will emerge from that gaping hole. And God's fire. Now there is none. No flame. No orange glow to warm the Tower, to bring life where none was before. This battle has raged for many ages, and here now it shifts to my field. Here to become a player on the board. To take up arms for my God. Yes. To fight and slay evil. A holy warrior now. And so I must go on. For only in the presence of God, only upon the blessing of his light, can I be made his archangel, and strike down this vile demon. And so I see it all now. All the truth of his quest. What I must recover and what I must wield. The holy, flaming sword of God. And so back in through the mall, to the destroyed lift shafts, the only way now for me to rise. And all my doubt now pushed back down. All those questions. They cannot go on. They cannot be allowed to torment me now, not at this point in my journey. Whatever the truth now, there is a reckoning to come. My God has been by my side all these long years. Whatever his true face, soon I will look upon it and I will know. So embrace my quest. And push on. Climbing up and up in the darkness, hand over hand, gripping to the cable. And trying not to look. Not to look down. For down now is the abyss, and what is climbing behind me is terrible. It must not be looked upon. It must not be acknowledged. To gaze at its form would be to render it solid. And then those hands. Those claws. Can almost feel the tearing and stripping of my skin. The peeling away of my soul. The intense searing as I am consumed by that darkness. An hour. Maybe two. Many. Until an open door onto a new level. And when I pull myself, exhausted, onto the floor, I am overcome by sleep. And it is a sleep of colour and shape. Of sounds I remember. Faces pushing into view and voices calling. And it is a happy sleep because they are all smiling and she is laughing. And she is throwing a ball in the gardens. And the sun is upon her. Now dragged out of sleep by the vibration in the floor, shuddering through my body, my teeth clattering. I bite my tongue. The Tower is lurching over to one side, more extreme this time. And again the crumbling and crashing of stone, and this sliding away. I have to scramble to avoid being cast into the mouth of the lift shaft. Falling down into the black throat. Now braced against a wall, my eyes clenched. Such are the prayers in my head. Such are the words I could once speak, but now can only hear inside. Make it stop. Make it stop. Make it stop. I am fear. I am churning sick of dread. And over the din of collapse, some other noise. A bark. And another. Dog. Now staggering across the hall. Here are the doors to many apartments. Here they are lined up and jumping in my vision, this constant shaking and rumbling of rock. I am falling along this corridor. I am walking on the ceiling, now the walls, now the floor, on my belly, dragging, my hands clawing, and the barking, and the raging Tower roaring loud and collapsing. Here the stone becomes dust. Here the plaster filling my mouth. Now the choking and the coughing up of the guts of wall. And the tumbling into this open door. And my desperation to find my friend. To not be lost and alone. Against a wall. Or maybe the floor. The turning of the building. The twisting architecture. What furious battle God is waging against the creep of the dark. The world shudders at their mighty blows. My body aches. Within me the bruises of their warfare. This mouth tastes blood. And the barking of Dog. Closer. Searching. Seeking. And I tumble into the hall, and his lithe brown shape slips into another doorway ahead. So now I go after, and into this place, and into the gloom, into his excited yelping and leaping. Now the battle subsides, and the air is full of dirt and smoke and ash. And we are together. And I have my friend. He is not lost. I am not alone. And so I hold him close and he nuzzles into me. And I have no ball to throw for him. Here is an apartment I remember. Here are the rooms that were my home. Before. This is the living room where I read. This is the bathroom where I washed away the dirt of the mine, never quite scrubbing away the black of that rock. This is the bedroom where I slept, and where, for a time, she spent her nights, reading my books, revelling in words and language. Unaware of God's looming wrath. This is where my father, drunk and old and raging, blamed my mother's death on my leaving. And for the first time in his life, he hit me—a limp, pathetic slap that stung inside more than it did outside. And he howled and sobbed like a child. And all I could do was watch him crumble. It is all empty now. This was the site of the first cleansing. This was the first place to burn. And here I stayed for many years after. My nest of blankets lies still in that corner, surrounded by the crude faces drawn on the walls, carved into the plaster. Those white outlines against the blackened canvas of wall. All the same face. All the same blank eyes. Amongst my own bedding we gather ourselves. Dog stays close, unwilling to part again. And my hand to that face. My fingers gentle, shaking. To trace those features again. To touch the smooth skin, lips. And the warmth of her, as intense as any fire, burning bright. Yet unreachable. Uncontainable. So my hand falls away. And my heart beats in my chest. My lungs draw in the musty air. And these are things she will never do again. And I know who I have to blame for that. There is a low, almost imperceptible rumbling through the building now. Like a racing pulse. Something caged and waiting for its chance to be free. To be unleashed. And it is more than just a sound. It is in the walls. In the fabric of the place. Like a skin over everything, throbbing, as though hidden just below veins are coursing. Adrenaline pumping. Muscle and sinew braced for sudden movement. For a terrible lunging. Dog feels it too. His eyes are wide and staring. He glares around, at the walls and at me. His small body is tense. And as I feel him breathing, his body against me, so too do I breathe, in time. And, most terrifying of all, synchronising with the breath of whatever lurks. We must move. We must go on. Yet so tired and pained. This body is wreckage. This mind so fragile now. To go on may be to go to my grave. What an end it would be, though. At the side of my

God. For I have done all He has asked. To fall now would be no shame. But what guilt would remain, as a blight upon my soul? To be pursued to the end by stain. And so we go on. And the collapse of Tower is around us. All strewn rubble and fallen masonry. Exposed framework, cabling. The plumbing of this building, spilling a foul effluent. This bleeding building. So paranoid here. Suspicious of every turn and corner. Every rise and stair. For this building may be transforming. A sudden and catastrophic change taking place, surging up from beneath. A virus taking hold and rewriting the history of my home. My world. And so now those veins pulsing beneath the skin of wall are horrifying conduits of disease. A network of rhizomes reaching up into the Tower from underground, both feeding on and injecting into. Fire would cleanse this place. Some holy maelstrom. With the holy artefact gifted to me by God, I would fight this. Here and now, I could end this. And yet the artefact is lost now. Fallen into a place no amount of searching could recover it from. And so I was left to tend to its absence. To the wreckage in its wake. Only one was strong enough to carry that dense blackish silver ball. Only I was chosen for that task. The voice of God. And so it is that only I can wield the light, the sword in God's name. Such is my fear of failure. That on lifting that blade, I will falter and fall, burning. Like so many others. But no, I will not fail my God. This all must end. Through those dark tendrils I will slice.

Into the heart of this encroaching abyss, I will strike. I will burn it all away, bring light into that blackness. And all will start anew. All reborn. How much farther? How many more floors? For hours, the stairs and the hallways, these rooms, all empty shapes. All a reminder of the absence. And how will I look up on the face of God? Will I meet his eye, as an equal, or avert my gaze? Those who tried to hear his voice were consumed. Would I be any different now, upon staring into that light? And yet to be incinerated in that gulf of fire, would be to rise beyond this plane. To become truly angelic. The cleansing of fire.   And now there are no more stairs to climb. There are no more lift shafts open and free of collapse. This is not the peak of the Tower, yet it is as high as we can climb. All passages leading up are blocked. Choked with great lumps of black rock. These hands work to free them. Like the days in the mines, pushing and beating, but with bare fists, blackened and red with my blood. And a rage. To be thwarted at this point. My roars reverberate out of phase with the building's anxious shivering. I am mess of pointless noise and anger. My frustration. My body a quivering, eager to lunge at something. Yet this building remains impassive. Unyielding to my useless blows. And so over the skewed floors we find a balcony, a promenade up here in the highest point we can go. Here we rest. And here I bleed. Dog, perched at the edge, his brown eyes cast down into the far below. Now a hollow that stretches beyond the ground, and into the terrible dark. And he just stares. This body lying. No more strength left. No more energy. No more. This is where it ends. This is where the climb must cease, and the failure becomes real. This is where shame and guilt— Where blood and tears. Aching muscles and worn, ragged body. This is where I await my God. For I cannot go on. There is no more on. What lies above me here is unknowable. How high here, I do not know. I cannot see below. And I do not want to see. For what crawls upwards towards me now, what spidery legs cling. Such a deliberate, slow progress it has made. And at last, soon, it will be upon me. And, in my final moments, I am far too weak to resist it. And yet my toxic guilt, my sin, will surely do for it as it has done for me. So to die with purpose. So this body a weapon. This soul a poison. And this is God's plan, after all. Only through time does the mystery reveal itself. And I cannot fight it. I cannot question it. Lying here as sacrifice. An ultimate gesture. And I will be reborn in God's light. Welcomed as a new man. Forgiven. I wonder what Heaven is like. I wonder if the people I once knew are there. For sinners though they were, God's compassion is absolute. And yet I did not always think so. For many years they were the condemned. The betrayers. Was I wrong to cast them in such a role? And what shall I say to them? On seeing their faces again, how shall I explain the decisions I made? The actions I took? How can I make them understand it was for their own good? And on that day, the holy artefact was lost. From the plaza below, now collapsed into the deep, it was thrown. Many people were angry. They raged and rioted. Stores were ransacked and the windows smashed. Fights were everywhere. Work in the mine had long since ceased, and all the men, too sick to work, sought out something and someone to blame. And some took to the deep tunnels to find safety and shelter. Yet they found only their own burial. And I searched for her. But she was lost. Taken from me by the ravaging that was eating through the Tower. So I was to throw myself from the plaza. Truly my lowest point. With nothing but the emptiness ahead of me if I lived or if I died. I stood upon the edge of the walkway, the holy artefact in both hands, the voice of God coursing through me. Such sweating moments they were. In a daze of shivering and heat, the intensity of his voice burning through me. It was as though light was leaking from my very body, out through my mouth. I felt, in that moment, as though I were a conduit to God. And yet I had not reckoned with the power which I channelled to earth. And so they found me. They dragged me to the ground and beat me. Their words, cursed, vicious words, cut my body, cut my soul. A furious barking of rage. Senseless language, of pure hate. Lying there, suffering the kicks and blows, knowing death, at ease with the inevitable. Giving in. And letting go. So they took it from me. And as they screamed in pain as the power of God seared their skin, the artefact tumbled through the air and arced over the balcony. Some chased after it, falling to their deaths. Most stood in horror as their people cried in pain at their blackened skin, or wailed at the loss of an object even they knew was of great power, even if they lacked the understanding or the ability to wield it. And I watched as it seemed to hang in the air for painfully long moments. Then it dropped like lead. And God's artefact was gone. For many minutes there was just the empty silence. Then the return of their wailing and crying. The shouting and demanding of answers. Their questions and accusations, thrust in my face, spat at me and punched. They dragged me to the edge and threatened to throw me down after it. And I begged them to, for I had lost the thing that God had entrusted to me. His blessing upon me, stolen and thrown away. Such a failure. Such a false prophet. And the light came in a flood. The ground shaking and rumbling. And at once there was an enormous crack, and the air full of the sound of millions of angry bees. And all the people a confused mass of alarm and panic. They let me go and ran to the balconies, to look down to the gardens. And as I crawled to the back of the plaza, my body felt the presence of God. And everything burned. And what was left, I tended to. As was God's will. Many times I stood by the fire, or watched it from the higher floors, searching for the glint of silver within the orange and snarling yellow.

Thoughts of dowsing the fire, to retrieve it. Or of walking into it myself, as the flames did not harm me that day. God would protect me, surely, in reclaiming what was his blessed gift? Yet the heat was real. The burn was real. And so it remained lost. As was God's plan. A plan that has brought me to this day. To this point. So high I have risen. So far travelled. And not just in the climbing of the Tower. My whole life leading to this point. God placed me in the mine on that day. He placed the holy artefact there for me to discover, and only me. And through me, God's power was made manifest. And a glorious reshaping. Painful, yet a necessity. Yes. That is what I will tell them. It was necessary. And they will know it. For they too will be embraced by God.

And so here I will wait. To finish God's work in the only way open to me. Now Dog is sitting up. Now he is ears alert and looking down, urgent. I am frowning and sitting forward. This is it, this is the rising. My heart races, for now it comes for me. And this body must be ready for the end. Now he barks. And yes, here it comes. My eyes closing now for whatever creature or phantom is climbing for me, arms reaching, legs clambering. I am in God's sight. And yet nothing. Here waiting, but nothing. Just Dog barking into the void. I drag myself to his side and peer down at the wreck of the Tower's inside, the great chimney. The throat. There, far below, the yawning chasm of black, spewing out the rot. But I sense a stillness. And Dog is

silent and still now. A whine. I
hold my breath.

What has risen may sink, and what has sunk may rise.
H.P Lovecraft, *The Call of Cthulu*

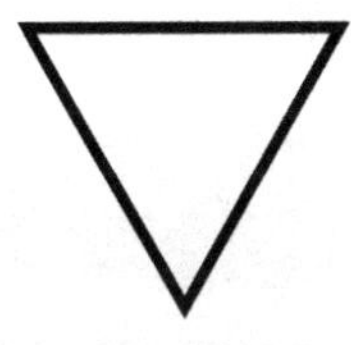

THE WOMAN OF THE DEEP

this abyss am am the abyss am the dark the
deep the void am endless forever inside am
the deepest place yet inside is a place deeper
even collapse into that void fall forever

alone and the wanderer all are dead maybe lost
in the dark don't make the noise they used to
are fallen crushed drowned are dragged down
by their own fear

no fear no more once cried into the nights once
clawed against the rocky walls and wailed
voice trailed into the imperceptible dark left
brought here to die won't fall be crushed or
drowned will choose when and where will
show

how long how many years what does it matter
time has no meaning there is no sun no stars
no sky only vast rocky ceilings arc over in the
pitch can't see them but feel their weight feel
the pressure of so many layers

time is a measure of anger the longer the years
the less the fire burns until it fades and only

embers smoulder fire never truly dies and while it may glow there is still heat there is still

am only now am only the present all that was is faded and decayed and echoes are lost in the deep places what lies before is unseen all is darkness and hands reach and fumble grasp at air cling to the rock through this earth prison of black dragging

and to reach something to find somewhere to just lie here and sleep what is sleep am not alive or dead feel the air on face feel that movement against skin so to follow and rise to emerge into day or night or something to remember rain to remember sun what are these things now here is empty here is void am within and around am

stories told of this place remember them well repeat them over and over mumbling lips in dry dust crawling men of work men of men many lines of them again and again descending but never finding what lay within never seeing their hollow insides father with his tales the rocky rust and stench of sweat his bushy beard his laugh and barrel chest hands that held and held the world what good is it to cry for the lost no tears here the tales are told to remember the why and the how to hear words and remember shape

he was strong father crushing arms of the miner a life of drilling dragging destroying carts of rock push and pull so heavy but am strong am mighty in this pitch father would be proud of his daughter he would see and smile

but am tired so much to do so much work and strength is leaving how old am what is age worn and ragged as am near spent am still smouldering embers

here are words here are tales told to hear and remember to repeat until all those words are one sound consumed by the drawing down of light into the deep

father worked this rock his whole life his father before and so on back into the ages down into

the depths their voices he told the tales his
father told him told him by his father those
tangled stories so intertwined lost now like am
impossible origins

It is said my grandfather was an albino. The other children taunted and teased him. White Eyes, they'd call him. At school. At play. A sickly child, my father said, always falling and hurting himself in the gardens. But when his time came to descend into the mine with the others, with those same school friends, a man he became. And they all saw him in a new, powerful light.

He grew strong in the dark. His size, a source of his clumsiness as a youth, now earned him the popularity he had always craved. And so a totem he became. A good luck charm, brilliant alabaster in the pitch night of the deep tunnels. They all wanted to be by his side in the dark, my father said. His mighty stature. His mane of white. It is said that his body glowed in the dark as the sweat poured from his brow.

And when there were cave ins, which were many in those days, he was the first to throw himself into the search for his comrades. His huge hands digging. Throwing large boulders this way and that. Ploughing through the collapsed earth. His determination written in great arms swinging to clear debris. This once thin, sick child, now a legend walking.

And so when he met my grandmother, they were married quickly, for he was a popular young man. Admired not only by his fellow workers, but by many of the young ladies looking for husbands. There were whispers though. That their children would be freakish. White ogres. Deformed. People are cruel, father always said. They would never understand.

Their wedding was well attended. The gardens full of people, dancing and singing, a stage erected for the miners' band. There was laughter and celebration, and the sun shone down upon them.

My father was their only child. But his father was already gone when he entered the world.

It is said my grandfather descended into the darkest, deepest regions of the mine. Into the oldest tunnels. It is said he found something. It is said he never died.

ancient halls echo the footsteps of albino
grandfather hands pulling through the dark
as am pulling would he shine as bright still
after so much time would see that shimmering
shape a beacon now leading to the light of
family

drag and push through the mine pause to listen
the great mouths of collapse the openings of
lift shafts wait sometimes for long periods of
time listen for him maybe down there crawling
around in the dark like am maybe just trying
to find way to the top

of the surface have no cares only the deep the
darkness of this pit now a cold empty womb
to nestle in

father always the clown grew up without
father the boy of missing many men went
disappeared in the depths was not alone so
invent a father create a fiction half-truth and
he told and tell it over and over and who's to
know where it begins and ends

what truth maybe father had no father maybe
truth he emerged from the mine as man grew
from rock then married mother and am the
daughter of rock this rock this deep black
growing into core of earth rock and am born
to return

as all things are

My albino grandfather walking into depths. Taking the lift down to the dark and pit. Down to the ancient halls no one goes to. Why? What did he go there for? What did he see? my father asks. It is said he often wandered down there by torchlight, reading ancient wall carvings, exploring lost tunnels and chambers. My father says that he went there to die, maybe. That being a father was a great burden, he was unprepared for. Such a mighty man, so strong and capable. Now lost forever in the abyss. Yet what, father says, what drives a man to do such a thing as his own child comes into the world? Other men figured him for a coward after all. Others that he found great deposits of gold. He ran off to the city to be rich. He lives in a grand mansion, has many wives. But no, father says. He is still down there. And my father says that he knows this because he has seen him.

Where? Where in the deep? Is grandfather lost, wandering alone in the dark? We must go to him and help him. And my father smiles and shakes his head. Something was found, he says. Something wonderful.

and say into the dark and ask the abyss what
was there what was found and the pit responds
such vast unyielding silence so will drag this
put it down the hall carry and shoulder and
body will move and the words on lips father's
words telling the story of grandfather the
white ghost of the mine

And so it was that within days of my grandfather vanishing into the deep, the men working the rock became edgy and tense. If one as mighty and well respected as he could be consumed, then who was safe anymore? Sinister talks of strikes. Unrest glowing hot under the uniforms and in the homes at night. The sound of my baby father crying out for his lost papa.

They searched for him, for sure. As tirelessly as he had searched for some of them, buried under fallen rock, collapsed ceilings breaking their legs and their arms. So scared to go deeper though. Yet a few who dared, they returned minus two of their number. Lost to falls and to flood waters in the deep. And sounds they heard, for sure. But was it him? Was it White Eyes?

Of that they could not be sure. The sounds they described more like that of a beast. An animal. Something breathing down there in the dark.

And my mother a widow with a baby to raise alone. My father tells of her as a broken woman, fragile and delicate. Forever hoping that her husband would return to her. And as long as she lived, the tales of his subterranean wandering reached her. And my father's friends taunted him, the boy of a missing. The boy of The Missing.

She was sure he was alive. She took that belief to her grave. At the funeral, father said he watched the faces gathered, hoping one would stand out, that one would make itself known to him as his lost papa. He laughed though. How could he ever know way down there in the dark? How could one wandering so far from home ever know that his loved ones were suffering?

like am way down here in dark what
movements above what developments long
since have no thoughts no messages reach no
voices

and yet

sometimes ground shakes above is a low distant
rumbling of walls rocky hallways through am
crawling feel it move through hands and knees
often just very quiet very far away from above
not below nothing ever stirs below for a very
long time now it has shivered through the
mines each time stronger a beckoning call

and so follow move closer to dig out the
tunnels as move through hear father's words
from mouth miner's language of dirt and sweat
dragging and digging and am grandfather
surging through the black glowing white body
searing am reaching out to that ebbing rumble
am pulling towards it for grandfather for

am grandfather's child am the daughter of a
missing the missing am furious white lost in

deepest dark forgotten forgetting am father's
voice his words in mouth am the moving
memory of collapsing rock the movement of
earth the return

and father the seer one who sees his night
time tales of the deep mines of men and their
laughter to see daughter off to sleep into
dreams into daytime reveries what lurks in
the dark places what crawls on bellies pale
unknown to light

so in the abyssal halls grandfather's figure
takes shape a white spirit out of gloom
through the twisting maze of tunnels walks
an endless search for something and calls
out grandmother's name weeps for her in the
darkness he sits there alone and questions he
wonders why

So it was said by my father, that he and many other men heard the sound of that white giant weeping alone. It was said that, perched by this or that shaft, the delicate, distant sadness drifted up.

And those who heard that sound were left haunted. A melancholy that settled over them like a dark cloud. So they were reduced to tears at their work with the stone. They were useless to their comrades. Sent home to be with the women, since they behaved just as meekly.

Did they search for him? Did they pursue those sounds? For the men of the deepest mines are brave, but not so brave as to chase ghosts, they say.

And what ghosts lurk in the hidden depths of such dark places? So many years, centuries, men tunnelling and digging by weak light. With the collapse and the flooding, the intense heat and cold. And the loneliness.

News did reach my grandmother, and she was heartened. But it faded as the time stretched on. Cold, impassive time. Bringing nothing. And my *father tried to embolden her spirit, telling her that he would go and search. He alone would enter the deepest depths and look.*

And my grandmother begged him not to go. Not to leave her. Not him too. She wouldn't be able to stand it if she lost her only son to the same fate as her true love. Both husband and child, to descend and be consumed by the great mouth of the earth. Such a fate no family should suffer. Those friends of hers, those widowed and childless friends.

My father though, he was determination and positivity. His smile as he took my grandmother's face in his mighty hands and kissed her on the forehead. Telling her to fear not, his journey would be fruitful and he would return to her. A promise.

And my father tells it that the route down he took was the same his father took before him, when into exile he went. With a powerful lamp, and rope, more ready for this journey. My father, young and strong, though not like White Eyes.

His comrades by his side until the levels they would

not dare go below. Their faces masks. My father stoic. In the travelling down, into the womb of the earth. His sweat. His eyes wide. The pressure in his ears as he descends. The knotting in the jaw.

Those who watched him vanish from view spoke of how they never thought to see him again. They had lost another good man. One more missing. Another ghost to haunt the dark places. Another weird whisper.

And my father walking the deep tunnels as my grandfather. His lamp casting dirty yellow light only a short way, such darkness is resistant to warmth and colour.

what he saw what he found as grandfather
saw and found down in the dwelling dark

and pushing carts barrels am on belly pale
ghost now out of the sun for an age as father as
father's father and so

They say they found him after some five days had passed. Emerging from a long abandoned tunnel, naked. Caked in dirt and mud and filth. And he spoke not for another five days. Not a word. He lay and stared. He lay and slept.

And blind. Tunnel blindness, they said, caused by so long spent in the dark. His eyes staring. His face drawn and hollow and led by comrades from the mine to his mother's side. How she wept. How she held him close and wailed, though he could not look her in the eye nor tell her of what he saw.

He did not speak of those five days missing. My father's mother questioned and begged him. But he was a smile. He was a warm embrace and a silence.

father's words in mouth his tale though he
spoke not of those days

the cave sky moves and shudders a roaring
through rock and it roars through all of body
there is collapse there is breaking away above
is terrible noise so closer am and the telling
must go on as the rock is through the words
must be through also

the favourite tale he told the girl am the child
his words are many and his favours land in
places not ready for his laugh was mighty
when he told story of the giant as mighty as
the giant itself loud and forever

and hear it now barrelling through these halls
from own mouth the air pushed from chest

The giant was born special. Of majestic ancestry. A magic man, great and tall, as wide as ten men. Hands so huge, like shovels, like carts, like animals digging and ploughing. And the giant had a magnificent voice, which could be heard from far, far away. He could reach out and take the sun in his hands. He could swallow the moon.

This giant lived alone, for he had no family. No one to love him or for him to love back. He was miserable and sad.

He was born alone. His majestic ancestry left him isolated. All his kind were gone and forgotten. An ancient being, his past a fog. And so he looked one day to the sun, high in the sky and glowing bright. He asked the sun, why was he forsaken? Why was he alone?

And the sun told him that the age of giants had ended long ago, and he hadn't noticed. He was too selfish, too consumed by his loneliness, to see that time had moved on.

And the giant wept. He wept a vast ocean, from

which spread many rivers, pouring into lakes. The whole world over the waters spread until finally his sobbing ceased, and he sat on the shore of the ocean and saw all the fish and creatures of the deep swimming and moving through his tears. He saw how people came and cast nets, how they caught the fish and took them back to their villages. How they built boats to hunt the enormous creatures that lurked in the waters. He saw them lure those beasts to the surface, and then impale them with sharp spears. He saw as they were dragged ashore and sliced open, carved up. And the red leaked into the sand. And the ocean became red with the blood of those animals.

Full of sadness, the giant went to the moon. And he asked the moon, why was he forsaken? Why was he alone?

And the moon told him that the age of giants had ended long ago, that it was now a new time for the world. It was the time of men, industry, science. He was an irrelevance, not needed, and not tolerated. He should dig a hole and lie down to die.

And the giant raged. He tore a great rent in the world, and threw the dirt high into the air. When the dirt fell, a range of mountains criss-crossed the world, and between there lay a huge abyss, reaching down into the darkest pit.

Here the giant saw the people constructing towns and cities on the plains in the shadow of those mountains, the snowmelt running into rivers, which powered engines of industry. He saw how they felled the trees on the mountain sides, how they burned the wood and made fires that raged hotter than anything he had ever felt. And as their power and knowledge increased, he saw the people hammer, drill, blast into the rock of those mountains. He saw them dig into the living earth, retrieving vast quantities of treasures and stone to build their Towers higher.

So the giant stared into the pit he had torn into the earth. He saw the black depths, so still and peaceful. And he wondered how far it went. How deep? And if he were to descend, would he emerge somewhere else? Some time else? He wondered if this might redeem him, or take him to where the others of his kind now dwelt. He would no longer be alone.

So the giant packed his things and climbed down into the great crack in the earth. He climbed down out of sight of the moon. Out of the warmth and light of the sun. Out of the way of men and industry and science.

The crevasse was cut down into the earth. It yawned wide, opening into a blackness that consumed the giant entirely. He could feel it all around him, the cold touch against his pale skin. He shivered as he went deeper, clinging to the crumbling rock, his mighty breath swirling like wind through a gorge.

For many days he climbed down. And he grew tired, his hands aching, his muscles weary. How long before a fall? How much further to the bottom? Several times he looked back up, wondering how far he had travelled. To see the sun, the moon, a light shining down into the pit. But all above was darkness. A great ceiling of night, where no stars shone.

He had never experienced such prolonged, intense

night. Never felt an absence such as this. And he found himself muttering, begging, some kind of ritualistic incantation to who he knew not.

And all around him the darkness of the pit descending. All around him the surface of the rock, that black, immutable stone, with no glint or fissure. He thought of marble. He thought of onyx. Of precious stones and minerals, the kinds he once hoarded and eyed with glee.

As the giant climbed down, he felt no wind against his face. Such a stillness around him. Nothing stirred. He was the only living thing moving, the only thing breathing, making sound. And he brought heat with his breath and his beating heart. His sweat poured from his brow into the rent of rock.

He paused, clinging to the face of stone. For now he could hear the dripping of water. The echoing through the earth. So the giant put his feet down, touching solid ground. And he wept and lay on the rocky bottom, thankful for finally reaching the end. Thankful for the relief his body felt, wracked with pain, fingers bleeding.

So the giant slept at the bottom of the world. Curled around himself to keep warm, he slumbered soundly for an age.

And when the giant awoke, it was to noise and the air full of thunder. Great plumes of smoke, dust erupting from all around and falling. A blanket of fine ground black covered his body, and he coughed. His eyes stung, and he cried out at the noise to stop.

But it went on. And the earth around him shook so violently. And there was crashing and the crushing of rock. And the sides of the ravine in which he had slumbered shuddered and shattered, fine fissures snaking up and around.

Such a smell. A harsh, unnatural smell. And eruptions deep in the rock around him.

Never had the giant heard such sounds. Never had he witnessed such a terrible scene of destruction. This is the end of the world, he thought. This is the falling away into abyss of all that there is. To be ground up and crushed. To be chewed upon by the jaws of eternity. To be rendered ash.

The giant struggled to his feet, brushing away the collapse of rock and debris that had fallen over him during his sleep. He took to the great walls of his prison. Hand over mighty hand, to climb up and emerge once again in the light of the sun and the moon. How he would be glad to see them once again. To feel the warmth of the day and the cool of the night. The stars and their bright shining tableaux.

But those walls roared angrily as he climbed. They shook and they crumbled. His mighty hands found little purchase on the broken rock faces, those cliffs climbing so high and far, and he knew he would never reach the sky again.

And so the giant fell. And as he hit the ground, a violent shudder erupted through the deep, and the black rock around him fractured and fell, burying him where he lay, weeping that he would be alone, and forever trapped staring upwards, always searching for the sky.

The giant remains at the bottom of the earth, in the deepest, darkest abyss. Alone and forgotten. Alone and forgetting. He is ancient. He is struggling to be free of the rock, but is ever more becoming the rock. And when he moves and twists, we feel the earth shudder. We see the ground undulate and moan. And the men of the mine, they see their comrades trapped or crushed as the tunnels collapse from the giant's desperate attempts to free himself and ascend into light.

father's words a baritone in mouth drawing
out the tale drawing out the mystery relishing
the darkness and laughing

there hear it slapping back along the tunnel
echo returning to a hollow sound an imitation
of laughter an imitation of life

the giant still moves still breathes am giant
hands would crush these tiny carts smash
them and their contents would roar would
dismiss light return to dark feel complete by
the absence welcome the void

and as lie here and breathe in dark curled
around body to keep warm those are hands
reach for those are mighty arms looming out
of deep and open to

am not ready for the journey deep down is
much work left here so giant breathes and
struggles the world shakes move onwards

speaking these words voice hush now laugh
now whisper speak to these walls hear tales

they might hear mine share our stories and
what stories would this rock tell legends of
time and movement an endless crush heat
cooling void dark all and more moving hands
over cold slick wet surface home walls

now here become the walls become their
mouth and words to speak the tales witnessed
share history and many things they have seen
many faces and voices are ingrained in rock
have been absorbed into the fabric drawn
down into the very essence of earth into life
rock to gestate and grow something someday
to rise

now recall the face of father these walls see him
as he works as he strides proudly through the
mine with workmates sometimes are laughing
sometimes are singing always happy

he works he sweats he loads the carts full of
black rock he calls to his comrades as they haul
the carts to the surface into the light beyond
these walls

see him help his friends when they fall when
the walls sometimes collapse see him race to
their aid brave and generous works tirelessly
to rescue as father before him

but these walls mean no harm when they bury
the men beneath their weight of collapse the
rock has no motivation no feeling it is memory
and history the deep earth it impassively
watches all around observes the passing of
time

and day father entered mine alone walls were
watching saw his face set hard eyes dull and
fixed in darkness a lamp to cut through the
inky tunnels carried with him many things a
knapsack descending deep

For many days he went down, the walls say. He slept on the ground, covered by a rough brown blanket, his knapsack under his head. He dreamed, but the walls do not know of what, for they do not see into the minds of men. Yet he did moan and thrash in his sleep, calling out words that the walls do not understand. They are meaningless and mangled.

own   mouth   moves   around   barking   into
darkness

He did not use the various lifts used by the miners, choosing instead to take all the tunnels and passages leading down. And there were times he encountered fellow workers who stared after him, questioning looks upon their faces. And my father smiled and nodded an acknowledgement, walking on. Further and down.

Those deeper, more ancient tunnels, long abandoned due to their instability. Here my father made camp. Here my father began searching.

And it was observed by those most ancient places that my father drew a map. Before setting off to explore, he unfolded a large piece of dirty white cotton. He studied it for a time. He made notes in charcoal or pencil. He peered long into the darkness with his lamp, listening.

At times he stopped and stared at the walls themselves. Moving up so close, his face almost touching. He put his ear to the hard black rock. His breathing. His pulse thundering. And when he cast the yellow light of his lamp upon the surface of these walls, he found markings and engravings, and his face beamed. He would crouch and take out his map.

For many hours my father made notes and rubbings and drawings. His sweat. His clammy hands in the heat of the deep places.

My father reached many sections of great collapse. Enormous gaping holes in the earth that appeared bottomless. Such pure void. Immense abyss. He called down into those places, and his voice was lost. No echo. No return. Just swallowed up and forgotten. Or perhaps stolen.

And so he would sit by those incredible depths and study his notes by the yellow light of his lamp. Muttering words that I cannot repeat. So twisted. So unknown. They come to me from such dark and deep realms, compressed and squashed. When my lips move to make those sounds, there is a sharp pain in my head. A fire raging.

so these words of father incendiary are
blackened and charred like rock am cocooned
in so intense and unknowable without
meaning without purpose if put ear to these
walls would hear only the pounding of blood
then below that the hiss the searing the fissure
of sound that is this deep

father's words were not always as impenetrable
the hushed whispering use for the secret tales
he told the ones mother disapproved of terrible
and horrific

these words like creature and beast and dragon

and when they leave mouth those words shatter
against the stone the great tremors shudder
through the dark hold for long moments of
screaming the terror grows the feeling that am
ever closer to where need be

they forbidden words rarely do tell these tales
of what lurks in deep but have much power
much that is needed within

There is something that dwells in the quiet and the dark of the deep mine, my father would tell me. Something huge and terrible and white. It has existed for eternity, and will exist long after we are all gone. It will breathe and sleep and eat. It will endure because it is ageless and not made of the same materials that make up this earth.

All of the miners know of it, he would say. Some make offerings. They worship it in the dark, quietly, to themselves. They hope that if they please it, then they will be rewarded. A major find. A rich vein of mineral. Most hope they will be spared a horrible death, crushed under the weight of the earth, or drowned in the flooded chambers below.

And yet the miners do not speak of it. They will not openly acknowledge that it even exists. They hear it. They feel its presence.

Only a few claim to have seen it with their own eyes.

And my father's hushed words of that lurking thing. A creature coiled in the darkest tunnels, in *a chamber all of its own. There it sleeps, its great white body shimmering, sparkling like the night sky it will never see.*

When it wakes, it yawns. A maw as black as the void, opening into the white belly. And a rank stench. The glint of teeth. It knows of the men who work the mines. It can smell their sweat. Their fear.

So it slithers through the dark. That bloated body pushing, sliding over the black rock, through those tunnels so far down.

And as it moves, the walls of the caverns stretch and splinter. Great groans and gasps of earth shudder through the mine, and the men hold themselves in terror. What they fear more than anything. More than being crushed or drowned, or falling. The fear of being trapped alone. The dark. That silence stretching forever before them.

And those that saw. Those that survived. The few. Those that will talk, even fewer. Their blabbering and nonsensical gibbering words. They speak of something huge and white, with grey, sightless eyes staring blindly through the gloom. Staring blindly through them.

And for a time those who saw it were rendered incoherent. Unable to form words. Instead their mouths worked awkwardly, only a shapeless moaning emerging. It passed over the course of some days. Those who recovered returned to the mine warily. Their minds full of horror. And while their fellow workers believed and knew they spoke the truth, none dared talk of it. None shouldered the burden of fear with them. Those who survived and returned to the mine believed in silence, and were mocked by those not of the mine.

Those of the Tower. Those of home.

Merely myths and legends. Stories started by drunken miners. The loneliness and hard work of the mine. The dark. The long, unrelenting dark.

own dark own relentless void what stories
speak from own darkness what tales emerge
from this abyss am moving through and
becoming many a creature many a beast

So the walls watched my father writing. By lamp light in the lowest tunnels. His hands moved over the surface of those caverns. His hands made signs in the air. He looked to the high ceiling and he lowered his face to the floor. He lay there for a long time. Breathing.

And following this he slept fitfully. Sometimes the walls watched him sleepwalk through the halls. They saw him narrowly avoid shafts of complete darkness. They saw him descend waist deep into flood water, only to awaken with a cry. And he would carefully find his way back to his camp. To his light.

And the time came for him to pack up his things and begin the journey back to the surface. With a purpose in his stride. With a smile.

This despite his journey being a failure. This despite not finding his father. As these walls saw.

These walls felt something within them. They felt something surge and move and yawn.

and belly bulges breath is pushed from chest
with words of these walls gasp dry sounds
into dirt in deep feel something coiling and
pushing

My father felt it too. He stopped and stared as the tunnel around him shuddered. He was approaching a deep shaft, too old to have had a safety barrier that used to protect the higher floors. No more. He raised his lamp. His breath ragged. And the groaning. The deep roar of the earth. It drowned out his yells as he was shaken to his knees.

and yelling into the dark with hands over ears
the deafening roar of deep

And it rose up from the blackness of the lift shaft. Its bulging white body. Its grotesque shape. In the yellow light cast by my father's lamp, it waited. Those eyes moved. Sightless. Grey eyes.

clamping hands over mouth to drown out the
scream doing as father did those years ago in
the dark of deep repeating the tale

He stayed still as he could, despite his trembling, his terror. His unblinking eyes, staring. The sweat on his brow. His body drenched.

And the creature seemed to look straight through him. Those blind eyes mere clouded voids.

Yet my father saw the shimmering white. He saw the bulk of body. And his hands fell from his face. And his mouth opened to call out.

No words would form. A cloying clot of phlegm. And a cough. A choke. He spat into the dirt, and reached up to the creature.

It had descended back into its dark home. A silent retreat.

The walls felt that thing recoil. They felt it shiver and shake. And my father on his knees, staring into the shaft, calling out. Barking senselessly into the void.

in the dust mud of this empty chamber own
words empty and formless am blabbering now
am just rambling into rock into the floor the
walls the earth this stone taking in all these
speeches all these tales such a sponge of history
it radiates back to and am overwhelmed am
weeping for some quiet shouting out into
darkness dragging cart so tired so wasted and
berated and cart so heavy now

here stop breathe here start again the dragging
the scraping of metal on rock to stop some
distance crying with so much rage and
frustration and despair now on knees welcome
to sweet dark

and for a moment there is sound of another
voice not own not words of these walls or
father through own mouth another voice
distant and reverberating in the void

from above

heart racing thundering the pounding
incredible in skull stretching and breath

ragged and fractured hard to focus am so still
so can hear but this body makes so much noise
with breath and blood

wait hope and yet nothing a dream then a hope
foolish hope in the dark there is no hope there
is only an end

so to feet to take the strain of the cart to move
on to reach goal ahead not far

then thunderous crash ricochet slams wall
to wall floor to ceiling terrible cacophonous
clanging metal and stone slammed to the
ground hands to ears

and goes on as it falls goes on and on as
something crashes twists into deepest dark

here lie as sound dissipates into the below
quivering here hands to ears body a knot
feeling that thunderous descent through
bones and blood that cavernous roar through
the rock and through teeth grinding such a
ringing in ears

and it goes on for so long hearing and senses so
attuned to darkness can feel it falling still hear
it arcing and tumbling through the emptiness
above there would be silence now whatever
had fallen forgotten but feel the fall forever
it drags gut down feel that unending sinking
sensation all waters shift all blood

has been no movement above as long as have
been as long as have moved through the below
and so now this wonder

what has stirred from slumber by that racket
what is now awake and stretching that was
once dormant the thing that fell that twisting
tumbling metal it sends shattering shards
of sound through the very deepest places
whatever is down there whatever slept now
rising

that thing father saw that coiling mass of
white flesh all churning body and rank stench
through body feel it unfurl that abyss within
that darkness that throbs at the heart there it is
all a mass of alabaster terror unravelling itself

in the darkness of the soul within the darkness
of this cavernous below

as father lay in the dirt of the tunnel far below
am here shivering lips muttering of his struggle
to regain his voice to find his words amongst
the senseless noise that spluttered from his
mouth

These walls watched impassively. Watch me, with the same resolute lack of concern. My father had no idea how long he had been wandering, the words still not coming to him, slowly going blind.

Such is the power of this darkness, where sight is of no use. Like time, and memory, and history, and love. These things simply fall away, like the loose skin of some enormous snake. We wriggle in this void, to free ourselves of these unimportant hangovers. It is a process. An evolution. Eventually we all twist in the dirt and the dark.

My father was found by workers as he emerged from the gloom of tunnel mouth. Dirty yellow light washed over him and their words filled his ears. He was pale and wide-eyed. Unable to speak, only grunt and bark and groan. And he wept when they took him in their arms and carried him. They held his weight and they took him up into the light.

and beyond this deep beyond these walls and
so his tale ebbs and drifts from mouth until
only breath heaving into the perpetual night

it's the rumbling that pulls back to focus that
slowly intensifying movement pulsates from
the above only now so much more

work this rock must hammer and pick like
father like his comrades those who spent
lifetimes breathing in dark this dust who spent
life slowly growing blind slowly becoming
full of this deep with bleeding hands raw and
calloused with muscles worn and bones aching
am not alone and never have been the ghosts
of father grandfather their powerful arms and
hands they work with and through their song
fills lungs their hymn soars out of mouth

a folktale a myth a tale told by wives and
mothers sung at birthdays and weddings a
dance

The tale of a worker blessed with a great gift. Who found a buried hoard of gold and jewels while digging. Who brought it back to his home to show his friends and family, the woman he loved. Who was made greedy and arrogant by his new wealth. Who turned the community against themselves. Who introduced hate and intolerance. And who unleashed horror and violence when the woman he desired turned from him. When she could stand the sight of what he had become no longer. And so she was banished along with the others who had betrayed him. Sent to the wasted lands to die alone. And the lonely worker left with no one, to spend his remaining days in guilt and shame, drowned by the weight of his gold.

The melody always changes. Always shifts. Each new singer brings a new interpretation. I sing it as it was sung to me, by my father, on my birthday. With my mother clapping her hands and gleaming. Her eyes already failing her. My father's hand on her shoulder.

eyes gush with tears as work this stone the
song working through urging on pushing
and pulling the heavy metal carts loaded high
overflowing hands bleeding body aching

like so many workers before yet here am the
last the final alone what riches have what
wealth have found here only the vastness of
dark only the unyielding abyss and such is its
welcome that am the richest person to have
ever walked these halls

don't miss these people can't bring focus on
ashen faces burning blurs that sear that hiss
eventually fade away into darkness am empty
am devoid of light how the deep makes how
when enter this place are whole are light
full of blistering and blood growing through
the time of this place down in these hollow
depths ground down under pressure remade
in image of these halls nothing of the person
was is anywhere except these stories just these
words now

repeat them to keep them alive repeat them to

keep alive for without them am merely a shell
brittle and ready to snap a slight fall would
break a flash of light engulf in flames and am
not done here yet am not finished with this
place not finished with

so here lips move dirty and dry cracked do
these words even make sound any more is this
voice even heard hear it but how can know it
isn't like all the voices hear as unreal as the
whispering walls

to keep it alive to keep it moving pushing air
through the halls through lungs

and so the story of the boy who changed the
one made up self own it comes from within
the aching hollow of black and humming noise
inside it grew there over such a long time and
over so many repetitions so many words and
mutterings whispered it to the walls shouted
it into the endless halls screamed into this
vast void stood there and dared the beast to
confront begged to feel the heat of its breath
on face stood in place for such time teetering

on the edge eternal blackness beyond

the boy who was born with an itch in his soul
who from the day he awoke and looked upon
the face of his mother knew that he was born
wrong an itch that tugged at his skin made
him cry so much he wailed he screamed he
struggled when his mother exhausted put him
to her breast who thrashed all the limbs he
was born with and struggled for the words but
could never find them only raging and yelling
and noise

such an angry child and a mother who couldn't
cope a father who left embarrassed ashamed
disgusted so a child left to fend for himself
who never learned to speak communicating
in gestures and grunts and always the itch
the sense the knowledge that he wasn't right
but unable to speak it unable to explain and
so tears and fury and frustration spilling over
into violence fights with other children petty
crimes and intoxicants

the mother sitting across from her only child

in the prison visiting room her weeping
attracting the looks of the other wives mothers
a shared sense of despair disappointment
this son unable to put into words why unable
to explain just more weeping and snot and
thumping fists on tabletops

did he hate her then did she hate him for the
pain and suffering the trauma of worry for the
sleepless nights a frozen moment that look
those tears a mother's love and a son torn
apart by a soul on fire coiling within him like
searing oil

her turn to hard drink as she aged to deal with
the constant news of her son's raging of the
nightly calls from bars clubs dives prison cells
and wastelands how she aged and how the
bitterness of her own abandonment ate away
at her until all that remained was a husk of
a woman muttering to herself in her evening
years

the itch hollowed all it touched working its way
through the boy turned all that was inside and

good into emptiness and the mother and the
father recognisable only through his absence
the glaring hole in this family

and so on the morning of his ascent to manhood
this boy left the family home leaving behind
another void one which his mother would
never recover from

this boy naïve and wordless entering a city
of neon and noise so many bodies moving in
flashes of colour and sound vibrating the bones
in his body and here the people spoke so many
languages so many voices sounds within his
head a great clamour of words the image of
mouths moving and he understood for the
first time in his life he was able to discern sense
from that ocean of sound

still there the itch still there the burning in his
chest the knowledge that he was different born
wrong yet here was a place so full of colour
and light so he stood in those streets in the rain
in the night looking upon the enormous signs
on the buildings flashing moving changing

shape he saw how liquid was the colour how
light flowed and how when he looked up at
the sky there were no stars shining

here amongst the great tumult he was sure
was an answer so he put himself to work in a
bar he emptied ashtrays and collected glasses
he swept up and wiped tables he didn't need
to speak to anyone and no one spoke to him
but he could see all the faces of the city he
could hear all the words and gradually his lips
moved in those shapes

he practised long hours staring into his mirror
in the rented room above a laundry staring at
his face at his mouth pushing it into the shapes
he had seen those round movements those
jaws twisting and he breathed he pushed his
breath through his teeth through his lips to
make sound

every night after work he stood and made
shapes with his mouth pushed his tongue into
the sides of his face and breathed sighed and
his breath misted on the mirror glass and there

he saw the words he copied from the neon
signs blazing outside his window

those shapes so unfamiliar to him feeling so
unnatural yet with each day that went by more
came to him until he knew enough to open his
mouth and speak them to say his name

that sudden flush of blood through his body
when those sounds left his mouth when his
lips moved and he felt the weight of each
word felt it as a tangible thing from the edge of
his teeth they fell soft and round and fatty so
unlike the sharp angular noises he was used to
and he laughed in the street of neon and rain
he stood laughing

he spoke his name to all the people he saw as
he cleaned tables and collected cigarette butts
most ignored him others replied with words of
their own cutting barks he didn't understand
but desperately wanted to and even though he
sensed the aggressive tension in those syllables
he knew the power within them and wanted it

and when he saw her sitting alone in the bar
that evening he walked over and repeated the
now perfect set of words he knew and she
smiled and she glowed and he felt the warmth
of her

he had seen her there many times always alone
and sitting in the semi dark of the bar some
shallow white light upon her hiding her face
the first woman he had seen who aroused
mystery and wonder within him for she was
silent and bright eyes piercing as though
seeing through his very skin

she taught him new words she giggled them
to him over the bar her breath a sweet gush of
alcohol laced air her dirty blonde hair over one
eye her set angular face and jawline she was a
petite boyish creature dancing between tables
in the half light of that half place

from her he learned the language of the sky
of the neon and blazing city light from her
he learned the angry words the cursing the
hand gestures to go with them how powerful

those words felt on the tongue how scorching then the words of the body of sex together intertwined in her one room apartment bathed in shimmering white light cascading from the tableaux of giant smiling faces and words high as a building into his ear she whispered and those sounds vibrated through his body starting a fever that churned and twisted inside him

and through her window he saw all the words of the sky written in vast letters of light and he understood them then as his body felt the heat and the cold of red and white light the blinking the flashing the shimmering and all the power of language moving through him and all it could do

so he told her of his itch of his burning knowledge of his own difference and he struggled to make the right words to make a feeling so long unspoken suddenly understood

he spoke for such a long time for hours he paced the room back and forth scratched at his body clawed at the walls and when he lay down on the floor in the pool of flickering white light she lay down beside him and her cooling hand on his sweated brow

no words it took that moment for him to understand that sometimes they weren't needed a lifetime of noise of meaningless raging sound from his mouth and now in her tender white arms he understood that silence said just as much as any word he could ever learn

this boy becoming and full of words before his mirror in the mornings the same rehearsal as always working his jaw around those vowels only now a change subtle but there a softening of his face a shift in the character of his stance and within him the fire searing within him such yearning as never before

she saw it too when she peeled him of clothes and made him naked before her she admired the shifting contours of his landscape her hands moved over him and the city light cast him in such exhibition

she gleamed at him she was so happy and he knew it and could feel it that strange unfamiliar warmth he longed so much now to be within it forever always within that light

the more he learned the faster the progress of changing they walked the streets of the city together arm in arm pointing and singing aloud all the words all the things they saw together two young boys with their grins and excited laughter so they attracted the jeers and shouts of the ignorant the callous and they learned new words some she had heard before they stung and confused him and so tearfully she explained

perhaps once he was that person once he was that blind and lacking in humanity that he would shout or even assault those he saw and didn't understand so he wept and she cradled him against her

his hair grew longer his skin grew smoother

his lips became full his jaw softened his breasts
swelled his sex transformed

until the morning he stood before her naked
and washed in the static white light and he
was no longer he and she took her in her arms
and she kissed her and together they were as
one making a fresh geometry forever within
that light

the tale of the boy who changed the story full
of words full of sound full of light and shadow
and the city all bleeding out mouth spitting
dirty and rock dust and breathless as push
carts and heave rubble hands cut up bound
healed and cut healed again so much rough
scar tissue is that all am how much is left how
much is unscathed after so long tumbling
through the darkness of these tunnels

this is the space move towards this is the void
hammered and blasted and dug towards such
a pocket of cold and dark within this dark
void and though can't discern one dark from
another nonetheless sense all this space and

height feel the blackness the hair on arms
bristles

here now is home within these hollowed
out walls this womb in rock dug with hands
hammer father's words burning searing
through rock smell the char feel the heat here
will curl and slumber like some terrible dragon
coiled and waiting coiled and waiting

and around will be packed full no space left
no gaps will lie within the centre of it all and
forever sleep and here descend too far down
too far below a pale hand will reach up and
take down forever within that dark

but first must make this space clean and clear
all debris and clutter pushed and swept away
out into the halls and shafts to fall and collapse
in the unyielding dark

as if feeding the mouth of the abyss that
creature far below pale and grey eyed unseeing
in the never world it lies and with its mouth
agape turned up towards the sky of rock all

the abandonment of this upper world pours
down into that hungry maw

that great world eater the devourer of matter
objects touched by light and made hard
churning now within its great belly this mine to
make the heat that moves through those veins
and halls expelled in its poisonous breath the
wind on face

and as each cartload of rubble is tipped into
the throat of the mine as each torrent of rock
and earth and metal crashes and spins urge
that thing to rise rise rise consume all the light

these hands scratch and scrape reach ahead
and around over the rough uneven floor
into a wreckage of angles and sharp edges
enormous boulders and fractured faces of rock
disintegrating into dust in lungs

all into carts all moved with force of will or
blasted to fragments shattered then swept and
brushed away like a mother would

nothing here is soft nothing is curved or
smooth other than things crafted by those now
long gone and yet hands now reaching into
the mess of twisting and broken earth fingers
curling around something spherical

something round

a cry ricochets around the chamber a cry from
mouth and drop the object in fright a dull thud
no echo as thumps to the floor and scrabbling
away to a corner muttering and whimpering
legs thrashing at air

and in the gloom of own unseeing eyes the grey
shape of that orb looms large silver tinged and
catching light arcing strangely and blink hard
dazzled

some long moments of searing terror in this
darkness and try to push through the wall
through the floor scratch at the rock and when
scream there is the sharp taste of blood in
throat but can't really hear the sound because
there is a roaring like that of a waterfall in ears

the thunder of blood

and of being totally consumed by light what
fear there is inside a great blossoming dread
of harsh white expanding filling the void with
its heat reducing all to ash and scorch burning
away all this dark

the song of mothers returning now to tongue
screaming and yelling each line as if the words
would keep at bay that circle of grey hanging
in blind eyes

only there is no heat there is no light touching
skin bringing warmth where there is only
the cold and breathing slowly and moving
towards that sphere with reaching hands
fumbling through picking out

so long since hands felt something lacking the
sharp defined edges of rock unfamiliar with
this softness here in hands cupped this dull
weight impassive empty a stone

yet unnaturally curved like

like father's boules like used by men in the
mines simple games used their tools and craft
and skills to round off rocks painted such an
array of colours can no longer recall them just
the words

and weekends spent with father the gardens
him teaching how to roll that smooth black
ball across the lawns the other men the older
men grandfather's men smoked gathered in
groups discussing matches each of them with
round coloured boules red black white orange
silver sparkling and shimmering in the light

the men would play their games in the tunnels
under the brilliant lighting from the mine
lamps rolled down those uneven tunnels
sometimes vanishing into the ink into the
beyond then searching the man who'd lost his
prize boules or even his claim venturing into
the deep to recover it so father would tell that
on occasion such men would never return
ghosts lost forever in that darkness searching
for their precious spheres those missing

each one tool worked from the black stone of
the mine the stone of home of earth deep this
hole this future this eternity

each one found by its owner a particular rock
of a certain size and shape of certain density

It's said that my father found his deep in the depths of the mine. That he discovered it there when he descended, searching, and found the creature. These walls have whispered of that solid rock. Of that time when my father, wandering speechless and lost through the underground, despairing and sure of his imminent death, stumbled across a pile of rubble by a shaft.

And yet it was no shaft forged by him or his men. Not tooled by hand or machine, but seemingly cut through. Seared through by something huge. And all around the mess of collapse, of that which was forced out of the void as whatever made it pushed through.

Huge boulders, larger than my father stood straight. Marbled through with the peculiar silvery veins of this rock. Across the ground, fragmented remains, shattered and broken parts of the walls and ceilings, the guts of the world.

And there amongst that pile my father saw it. Almost already perfectly spherical. Perfectly black but glinting silver in the vague lamp light he had remaining. Rolling it in his hands, the weight felt good, the density ideal.

My father knew then that he had a match-winning boules. With this he could dominate the league of his fellow workers. He could rise to the top. Be number one. And although not normally a man of competition, with this in his hands he felt something grow within him. Now he was a winner. With this he would be powerful. And the men would all respect his command of the game. They would envy him, instead of seeing him as the child of an albino. A freak.

He took that rock back to the surface, hidden away at the bottom of his pack. And during the wordless days that followed his return to the surface, he felt it call to him. He felt the potential within that sphere yearning to be let loose. And through him, as the instrument of all that energy. What things he would achieve. What amazing victories.

and hands moving over the entire surface of
that object in hands here in the dark wondering
if this here is father's own boules somehow
lost in the dark somehow now found by the
daughter returned to the spirit of those same
hands that wielded it

nothing from this rock only the same cold as
all other rock

The men my father knew, those he worked with, shared the dark with, they saw a change in him. An arrogance, an impulsive swagger that they didn't like. In their games he never lost. And so their resentment grew. They demanded to know where he found his new boules. They inspected it, weighing it suspiciously in their hands, passing it from man to man. They fixed him with scowls. They thrust fingers into his chest.

Men my father had known for years. For decades. Since he had been a child. Grown up together. Worked all those years in the dirt and the dark. Now harsh words and squabbling.

Seeing my father depressed and miserable. Each day his face long and saddened. And sometimes the shouting as he and my mother argued. The slamming of doors. The late-night rattle of locks and doors. Whispered apologies. A breath rank with drink.

No stories when I settled for each of those nights. My father's words used up, congested in my chest, polluted by spite and anger. Then the creeping through the dark corridors of our apartment, to see him sitting in the gloom, the boules balanced in his hands. And just staring. For hours it seemed, his eyes fixed upon that black lump.

Crying then, and led back to my room by my mother, suppressing her own tears. Not really understanding at that age how a marriage falls apart. Not really seeing how it was not only the darkness that kept my mother from seeing clearly the things before her eyes.

imagine now that father threw his prize boules
down one of the many shafts cast it back into
the very deep from which he had found it see
him standing and letting it fall from his hands
its descent black into vast black spinning over
and over for eternity maybe finding its way
finally here to maybe waiting there slumbering
as the beast slumbers until the daughter should
come along and waken it call its name into the
void

crying now on knees here in this newly hewn
chamber wailing for all that was lost and
seeing clearly all that lies before with mother's
eyes and father's words this

the walls of this place are roaring a rush of
noise the sound of rock and earth twisting
crunching they are telling to hurry to move
quick and know something is stretching the
earth something massive is pushing exerting
so much pressure

the chamber is ready and there are no more
stories this is the end of all stories beyond is a

wordless vacuum an eternity within the abyss the stomach of the great creature this

now piling the room full of the carts and wagons all those left here by father and men all those others now lost to dust and dark body working just like any man worked in this pit sweat and muscle and grit am burning fire in flesh am searing determination and body will move until the pain in its core is immense and then will move more only when ragged and wrecked utterly spent will it lie down and then

a lifetime in the dark a lifetime fumbling through these abandoned shafts and halls through the machinery and powders a lifetime as an engineer's daughter an understanding even in the absence of light and vision

a lifetime in the below a lifetime in the ground beneath that thing that Tower that black spike cracking the sky

these boxes of chemicals noxious powders liquids now congealed but still retaining their

explosive potency piled around this chamber
now high as that ceiling from wall to wall
coiling keeping close closer than any has been
for such a long time and so in this final dark
chamber and so here lie waiting

one hand clasping father's boules only
connection now that our words are no longer
any use and feel it feel the energy father felt
when first he grasped it cold silver black mass
the warming moving through hand and wrist
into arm and as these walls sing a hymn so
loud in ears the shuddering the shattering the
falling away of all that heat surging into core

and as it burns so brightly through me my
mouth opens and I call out his name I shout it
scream it into the void I call to the beast to rise
now from its slumber to awaken here finally
to rise and consume everything in its jaws of
deep dark so vast and boundless

About the Author

Kenny Mooney was born in Berlin when it was still divided by a stupid wall. He grew up in Scotland, England, and Cyprus. He is the author of the novella *The Gift Garden* and the novel *Desk Clerk*. He lives in York.

www.kennymooney.com